This book
belongs to

....

Hans Christian Andersen's Fairy Tales

Compiled by Vic Parker

Miles Kelly

First published in 2017 by Miles Kelly Publishing Ltd
Harding's Barn, Bardfield End Green, Thaxted, Essex, CM6 3PX, UK

2 4 6 8 10 9 7 5 3

Publishing Director Belinda Gallagher
Creative Director Jo Cowan
Editorial Director Rosie Neave
Editor Amy Johnson
Designers Jo Cowan, Rob Hale
Production Elizabeth Collins, Caroline Kelly
Reprographics Stephan Davis, Jennifer Cozens, Thom Allaway
Assets Lorraine King

ISBN 978-1-78617-316-4

Printed in China

British Library Cataloguing-in-Publication Data
A catalogue record for this book is available from the British Library

ACKNOWLEDGEMENTS

The publishers would like to thank the following artists who have contributed to this book:
Advocate Art: Ayesha Lopez, Martina Peluso, Christine Battuz
The Bright Agency: Louise Ellis, Kristina Swarner
Illustration Ltd: Laurence Cleyet-Merle (cover)
Pickled Ink: Lucia Masciullo
Plum Pudding: Mónica Carretero, Claudia Venturini

Made with paper from a sustainable forest

www.mileskelly.net

Contents

Hans Christian Andersen 10

JOURNEYS OF DISCOVERY

LOOKING AND SEEING

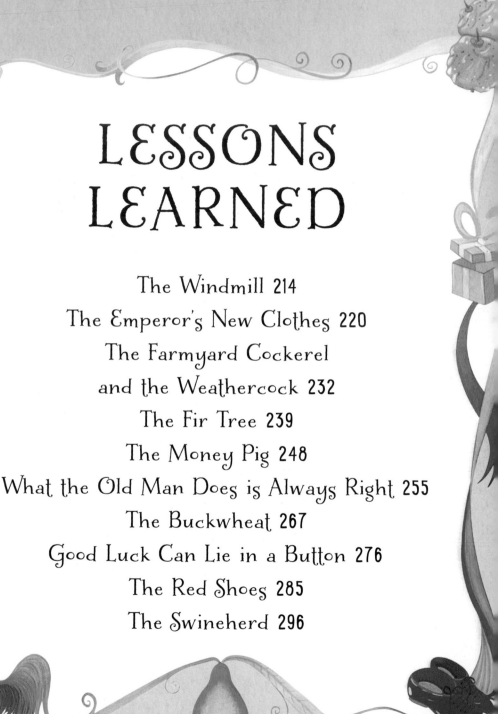

LESSONS LEARNED

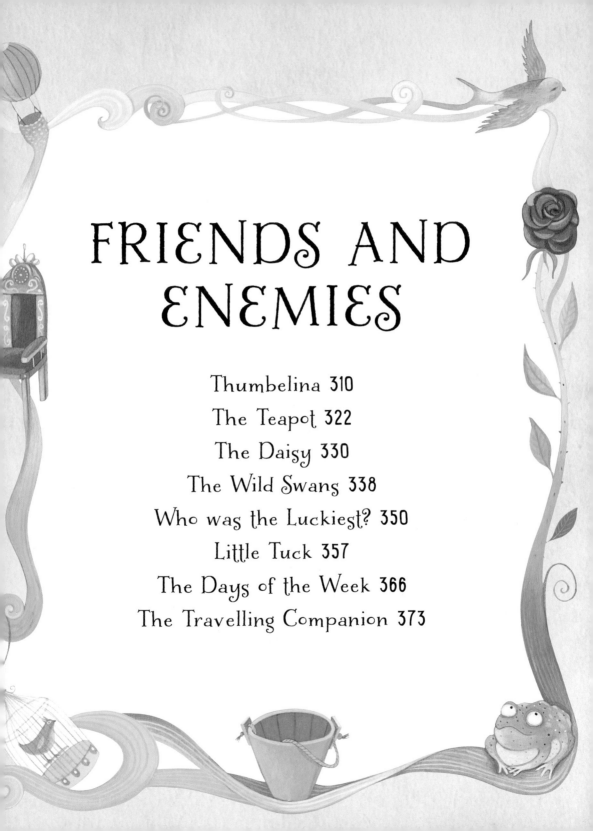

FRIENDS AND ENEMIES

Hans Christian Andersen

Once upon a time, over two hundred years ago, a boy was born in Denmark called Hans Christian Andersen. He was the only son of a washerwoman and a shoemaker. Even though Hans' family was very poor, his father took him to the local theatre when he could and made him toys. When Hans grew up he began working as an actor. However, he had a big imagination and soon found that what he loved most was writing.

Hans spent years travelling around Europe, learning about different places and people, and was inspired to write many poems, short stories and longer books.

Today, he is best-known for his fairy tales, which are loved the world over and have been made into films, plays and ballets. Here are fifty favourites retold for young children.

12

JOURNEYS OF DISCOVERY

The Little Mermaid

Far out in the ocean, where the water is as blue as cornflowers, it is very, very deep. There live the most lovely sea creatures and plants. In the deepest spot of all was a castle where the Sea King lived with his six daughters. The sea princesses were all beautiful mermaids, but the youngest was loveliest of all.

Every day, the sea princesses played happily in the castle or outside. Each mermaid had a little garden to tend as she pleased. The youngest mermaid grew flowers around the statue of a handsome boy that had fallen from a shipwreck. She loved to hear about the world above – for the sea princesses were not allowed to the surface to see it for themselves until they were fifteen. The little mermaid made her grandmother tell her everything she knew about ships, towns, forests, people and animals.

Finally, the youngest princess's fifteenth

birthday came. How excited she was to rise to the surface, light as a bubble! She raised her head above the waves and gasped as she saw a grand ship floating in the glorious sunset. The little mermaid swam close and peered in through the cabin windows. She saw lots of people inside, eating and drinking and dancing. Among them was a handsome young prince – it was his birthday party. As darkness drew in, the people came out on deck to admire magnificent fireworks bursting in the sky.

The mermaid watched, fascinated, until it grew late. But then heavy clouds gathered, thunder roared and lightning flashed, and the waves towered into dark mountains.

A terrible storm tossed and tipped the ship, until suddenly it plunged over on its side. Everyone was washed into the water!

To the little mermaid's horror, she saw the handsome prince sinking. His beautiful eyes were closed and she knew he was about to die. She dived down and used all her strength to lift him and hold his head above the water.

When the sun rose, the little mermaid swam to a sandy bay and laid the prince in the shallows. She stroked his wet hair and kissed his forehead – he seemed just like the statue in her garden. Then some girls came out of a nearby building, so the little mermaid hid between some rocks. She watched as one of them spotted the prince and ran to him.

The mermaid saw him open his eyes and smile. Then the girl helped him up and led him away.

The little mermaid swam sorrowfully back to her father's castle. From then on, her heart was filled with longing for the prince and the world above. 'I will see if the sea witch can help me,' she thought.

The way to the sea witch's home was very dangerous. It lay through whirlpools, boiling mud and poisonous plants. When the brave little mermaid arrived, the witch said: "I know what you want. I will change your fish's tail into legs, so you can walk on land and find your prince. But every step will be as painful as treading on knives – and you will

never be able to return to the sea and
your family again. If the prince falls
in love with you and marries
you, you will become properly
human, with a soul that will
live in heaven after you die.
But if he marries another girl,
at sunrise on the next day
your heart will break and you
will become foam on the waves."

"I will do it," said the little mermaid,
determinedly.

"But I must be paid," said the witch. "You
have the sweetest voice in the ocean. Give it
to me."

"So be it," the little mermaid whispered.

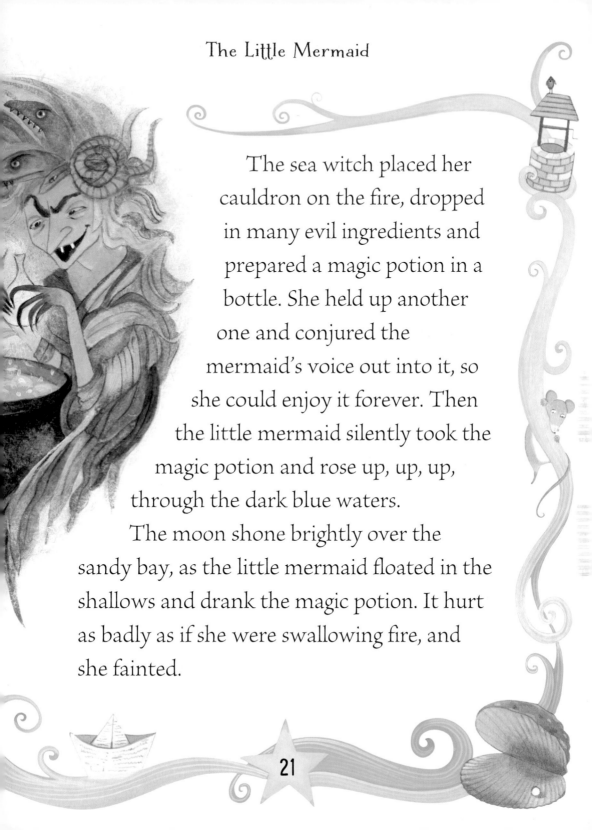

The sea witch placed her cauldron on the fire, dropped in many evil ingredients and prepared a magic potion in a bottle. She held up another one and conjured the mermaid's voice out into it, so she could enjoy it forever. Then the little mermaid silently took the magic potion and rose up, up, up, through the dark blue waters.

The moon shone brightly over the sandy bay, as the little mermaid floated in the shallows and drank the magic potion. It hurt as badly as if she were swallowing fire, and she fainted.

When the sun rose, the mermaid came to. She was lying on the sand and before her stood the handsome young prince, smiling. She looked down shyly, and realized that her fish's tail was gone. Instead, she had a pretty pair of legs and feet and she was wearing clothes. The prince asked who she was and where she came from, but the mermaid just looked at him sorrowfully, for she could not speak. He helped her to stand and walk, and every step she took was painful, but she didn't mind.

The prince took her back to the palace and looked after her, for she was the most beautiful girl he had ever seen. He was totally charmed by her and told her that she would stay with him always. The days passed and the little mermaid was overjoyed to be spending time with the prince – she only wished she could tell him.

But one morning, the little mermaid woke to hear church bells. "Today is my wedding day," the prince explained. "My father has ordered that I get married, to a girl who saved my life when I lay half-drowned on the beach."

The little mermaid felt as though her heart were already broken.

The wedding was held on a magnificent ship out at sea. The little mermaid was a bridesmaid and wore a gold silk dress. But she didn't hear the music playing or see the

colourful flags. Her mind was filled with everything she had given up, and of dying and becoming foam on the waves.

Late that night, the prince and his bride went to their cabin. The little mermaid turned to where the sun would rise and waited for the morning, when she was going to die.

As the first ray of dawn lit the sky, the little mermaid threw herself into the sea – but her body did not dissolve into foam. The sun rose and all around her floated beautiful transparent beings. The little mermaid suddenly realized that her body was like theirs, and she soared up into the sky.

"We are spirits," one of the beings

explained. "We fly around the world doing good deeds. When we have done enough, we are granted a soul and go to live in heaven. You, little mermaid, have been chosen to join us, as you gave up everything you held dear for love."

The little mermaid's heart was filled with joy. She left the prince and his bride behind her, and flew away with the spirits to win her soul and be happy in heaven for ever.

Five from One Pod

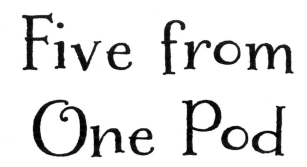

There were once five peas in a pod on a pea plant. The peas were green, the pod was green, and so they believed that the whole world was green. The pod grew, and the peas grew with it, sitting in a row.

Outside, the sun shone and warmed the pod. The rain watered it. And the peas grew bigger and sat there thinking.

"Are we going to be here for ever?" asked one. "There must be something outside – in fact, I'm sure of it."

A few days later, they felt a sharp pull at the pod – it had been torn off the pea plant. *Crack!* It was opened and the five peas rolled out into bright sunshine. There they lay in a little boy's palm. "You are fine peas – perfect for my pea-shooter," he said.

He picked one of the

27

peas from his hand and put it into his toy.

"Now I am flying into the wide world," called the pea to his friends. "Catch me if you can!" Then the boy blew hard into the pea-shooter and the pea was up, away and gone.

The boy picked a second pea. "I'm the biggest and best and I'm going to fly all the way to the sun," the pea called as he was slid into the pea-shooter. And away he went.

The boy went to pick two peas at the same time, and he dropped them and they rolled about on the ground. "Wherever we come to rest, we will go to sleep," they decided. But the little boy found them, slipped them into the pea-shooter – and away they went together.

Left behind, the fifth pea felt all alone. "Whatever is meant to happen will happen," he sighed, as he was fired out of the boy's pea-shooter. He flew up and away, until he hit a wall, just under an attic window. He landed in a gap between the bricks, which was filled with moss. The moss closed over him and there he lay. "Whatever is meant to happen will happen," he said to himself.

Inside the attic was a tiny flat where a poor woman lived with her daughter, who was not quite grown up. The woman scraped a living by cleaning stoves, chopping wood and other hard, unpleasant tasks. The girl could not help because she was very ill. She had been too sick to get out of bed for a whole year. Her mother was anxious that she might die. So every day, the sick girl stayed where she was, patiently waiting for her mother to come home from work.

Spring came, and early one morning the sun shone brightly through the attic window. The sick girl gazed out, enjoying the warm rays on her face – and noticed something. "Mother," she exclaimed, "what can that little green thing be that's peeping in at the window? It is moving in the wind."

Her mother stepped towards the window and half-opened it. "Oh!" she said, very surprised. "There is actually a little pea which has taken root and is putting out green leaves. However could it have got into this crack?

Well now, here is your own little garden for you to look at." The woman drew the sick girl's bed closer to the window, so she could see the budding plant. Then she went out to her work.

When the woman returned in the evening, her daughter said, "Mother, the sun has shone in here so warmly today and the little pea is growing so well, I feel I will get better too and be able to go out into the sunshine again."

"Please God!" whispered the woman, even though she didn't dare believe it. She used a stick to prop up the green plant which had given her child such hope, so that it would not be broken by the wind. Then she

carefully tied a piece of string to the window
frame so that the pea tendrils could climb up
it as the plant shot up.

And it did shoot up. The sick girl
watched the plant growing bigger day
by day. And each day she lay by the
window, warmed by the sun, and spoke
more cheerfully. She even began to
manage to sit herself up for an hour
or so, to admire the little garden of
a single pea plant that had grown
at her window.

One morning her mother
announced: "There's a flower
coming!" The girl had the strength to
stand up, lean out of the window a

little way, and kiss the pink pea blossom that
was opening. She was so happy, it felt like her
birthday. At last, the woman believed that

her sick daughter would recover. "Do you know," she said, as she hugged her daughter tightly, "I believe God himself planted that pea plant for us…"

But what became of the other peas? Well, the one who yelled, "Catch me if you can," fell straight into a gutter and was washed away by rainwater. The two lazy ones landed in the street and were eaten up by pigeons. The one who wanted to reach the sun fell into a muddy puddle. He lay in the dirty water for weeks, swelling up and getting fatter and fatter. "Now I am definitely the biggest and the best," he said to himself – just before he burst.

And high above, the young girl stood at

the open attic window with sparkling eyes
and rosy cheeks, thanking God for her
beautiful pea blossom.

The Shepherdess and the Chimney-sweep

There was once a sitting room in which there stood a wooden cupboard, decorated with beautiful carvings. The bottom showed a field of flowers and trees, with stags and deer peeping out. At the top was the sky, with clouds and soaring birds. Dancing through the middle was a little man with a long beard, two tiny horns and legs like a goat. The children who lived in the house called him Billy Goat's-legs.

Hanging on the wall opposite the cupboard was a large mirror with a table underneath. On the table stood a pretty ornament: a little shepherdess made of china. Her dress was pink, and she wore a red rose at her neck. Her shoes were painted gold, and so were her bonnet and crook. At her side stood a little chimney-sweep, also china. He stood holding his brush and a ladder, and was painted all over with smudges of soot – except for his face, which was clean and

handsome. He and the shepherdess had been placed so close together that they had fallen in love.

Another china figure stood on the table, much larger than the shepherdess and the chimney-sweep. It was an old Chinaman who could nod his head. He thought he was very important, because of his size. He acted as though he was the little shepherdess's father, always telling her what to do.

One day, when the family had

gone out, Billy Goat's-legs called out from the cupboard, asking if the little shepherdess would marry him.

The Chinaman nodded his head and Billy Goat's-legs looked delighted. The Chinaman said to the little shepherdess, "He will make a good husband. His cupboard is made of very fine wood, called mahogany, and inside is the family's precious silver tea set."

"I will not marry him. I would have to go and live in the cupboard, and I don't want to," said the little shepherdess, who was afraid of the dark.

"Do not argue," said the old Chinaman. "Tonight as soon as the family are asleep, you will be married to Billy Goat's-legs and go

and live in the cupboard." And he nodded his head and fell asleep.

The little shepherdess began to cry. "Let's run away," she sobbed, looking at the chimney-sweep.

"Yes, right now," he agreed.

"But how do we get down from the table?" the little shepherdess wept.

The clever chimney-sweep brought his little ladder to help her climb off the tabletop onto the table-legs. Then he showed her how to place her feet on the table-legs' carved patterns. And so they clambered down and safely reached the floor.

Just then, Billy Goat's-legs noticed them. "They are running away!" he cried out to the

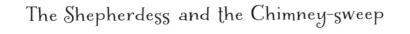

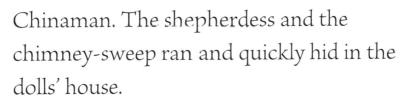

Chinaman. The shepherdess and the chimney-sweep ran and quickly hid in the dolls' house.

They waited, but nothing seemed to happen. So they tip-toed out – and saw that the Chinaman was awake and climbing down from the table.

"The Chinaman is coming!" gasped the little shepherdess. The chimney-sweep grabbed hold of her hand and ran to the log-burning stove.

"The quickest way out of the house is to go through the stove and up the chimney," he explained. "Are you sure you want to do this?"

"Quite sure," said the little shepherdess.

So the chimney-sweep heaved open the stove door.

"It looks very dark," said the shepherdess, peering inside. Still, she crept with the chimney-sweep through the ashes, up into the pipe and on into the chimney. Up and up and up they climbed – it was awfully steep – but the chimney-sweep helped the little shepherdess, and at long last they were out on the roof.

They sat down to rest. The starry sky was over their heads and below were all the streets of the town. They could see for a very long distance out into the wide world, and the poor little shepherdess leaned her head on her chimney-sweep's shoulder, and wept.

The Shepherdess and the Chimney-sweep

"I never dreamed that the world was so huge," she cried. "I am so frightened! I wish I was safely back on the table again… Please, if you love me, take me back."

The chimney-sweep tried to make her see sense, but she sobbed so bitterly that at last he had to do as she asked.

And so, with a great deal of trouble, the couple climbed back down the chimney, and then crept through the pipe and into the stove. They listened behind the stove door, to hear what was going on in the room. As it was all quiet, they peeped out – and saw the Chinaman lying on the floor with his head broken off! He had fallen from the table as he tried to chase them.

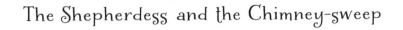

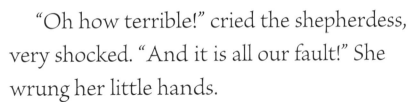

"Oh how terrible!" cried the shepherdess, very shocked. "And it is all our fault!" She wrung her little hands.

"Don't worry," comforted the chimney-sweep, "he can be glued back together. The family will fix him, I'm sure. He will be back to his bossy old self in no time."

"Do you really think so?" she said, brightening. And they climbed up the table and stood in their old places.

The very next day, the Chinaman was also put back next to them. The family had glued his head back on, just as the chimney-sweep had promised. He looked as good as new, except for one thing – he could no longer nod his head. So later on, when

Billy Goat's-legs called out from the cupboard, asking for the little shepherdess's hand in marriage, the Chinaman could no longer nod to agree. And the little shepherdess and the chimney-sweep remained together, living happily ever after.

Jack
the
Idiot

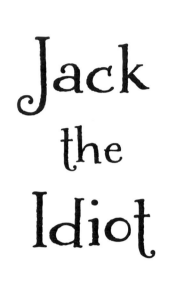

There was once a baron who had three grown-up sons. The eldest son had learned the whole dictionary off by heart. The second son had memorized thousands of laws. Everyone thought that they were both extremely clever – if rather boring.

One day, the king announced that there would be a competition to find a husband for his daughter. The princess would marry the man who was best at speaking to her.

The two eldest sons both declared: "I shall win the princess!" The baron was very pleased, and gave each of his clever sons a fine horse, so they could go to the palace and try their hand at impressing the princess.

As the baron was wishing the young men goodbye in the courtyard, his third son came out, whom everybody called Jack the Idiot.

"Where are you going, dressed in your best clothes?" Jack asked.

His brothers told him about the contest.

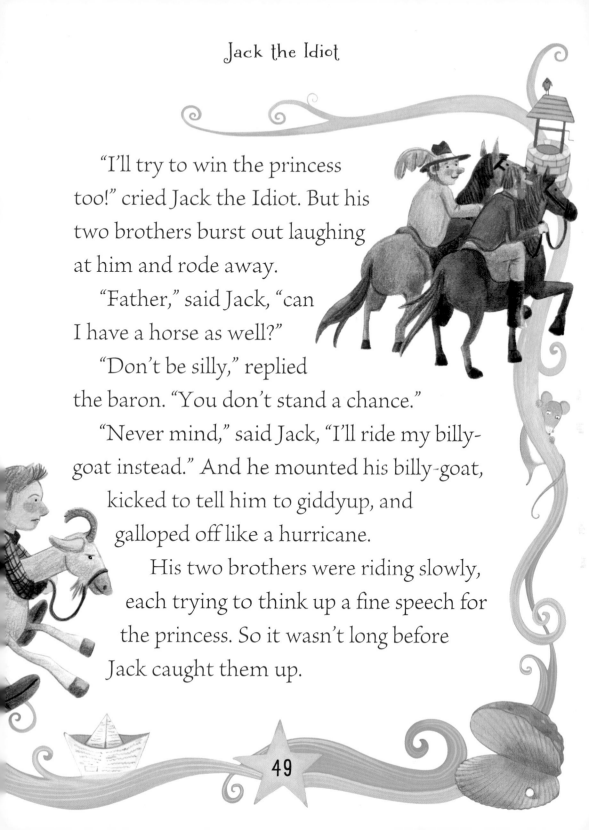

"I'll try to win the princess too!" cried Jack the Idiot. But his two brothers burst out laughing at him and rode away.

"Father," said Jack, "can I have a horse as well?"

"Don't be silly," replied the baron. "You don't stand a chance."

"Never mind," said Jack, "I'll ride my billy-goat instead." And he mounted his billy-goat, kicked to tell him to giddyup, and galloped off like a hurricane.

His two brothers were riding slowly, each trying to think up a fine speech for the princess. So it wasn't long before Jack caught them up.

"Hallooo!" he said. "Look what I have found on the high road." He showed them a dead crow he had picked up. "I am going to give it to the princess."

"Eurgh!" said the brothers, disgusted, and they all rode on.

Not long afterwards, Jack spotted an old wooden shoe and picked it up. "Hop-rara!" he announced excitedly. "I shall give this to the princess too."

And his brothers laughed and rode on.

A little further, Jack scooped some clay out of a ditch and filled his pocket with it.

"Don't tell us," the brothers scoffed, "that's another present for the princess."

"Of course," said Jack, very happily.

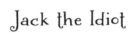

His brothers shook their heads and galloped off until sparks flew from their horses' hooves. They reached the town gate a whole hour earlier than Jack. There were hundreds of competitors there, waiting. Each one was given a number and stood in order to take their turn. Great crowds had gathered around the castle to catch a glimpse of the men and to see which one the princess chose.

Then the competition began. One by one, the young men were called into the castle and shown into the great hall. The instant each one saw the princess, he was so amazed by her beauty that he quite forgot how to talk. Each competitor stumbled and tripped over his words until the princess sighed and said,

"He is no good! Away with him!"

At last came the turn of the brother who knew the dictionary by heart. But as soon as he gazed upon the beautiful princess, he forgot it altogether! He grew so nervous that his thoughts whirled round in his head and all he could say was, "Um… er… my lady…"

"He is no good!" cried the princess. "Away with him!"

Then it was the second brother's turn. He was just as tongue-tied as the first.

"He is no use!" cried the princess. "Away with him!"

Next, it was Jack's turn. He rode right up to the princess on his billy-goat.

"It's abominably hot in here!" he said,

warmed by the huge fire that blazed away in the hall.

"Yes, my father is going to roast chickens later," replied the princess.

"Do you think he'll let me roast my crow at the same time?" asked Jack, showing the princess his find.

"With the greatest pleasure," said the princess. "But have you brought anything to roast it in?"

"I have!" said Jack. "The perfect roasting tray." He brought out the old wooden shoe and put the crow into it.

"Well, that is a great dish!" said the princess. "But what shall we do for gravy?"

"Oh, I have that in my pocket," said Jack, and he poured the clay out of his pocket into the shoe.

"I like that!" said the princess, beaming with delight. "You have an answer for

everything – and so you will be my husband!"
And that is how Jack went from being an idiot to a king, and lived happily ever after.

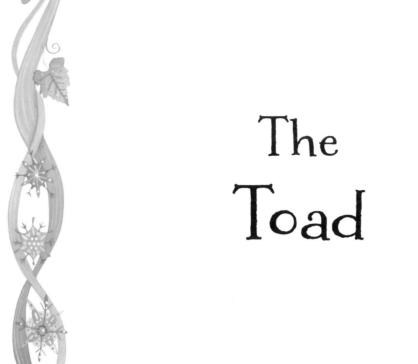

The Toad

The well was deep and dark – and home to a family of toads. They knew that the well wasn't the whole world. In fact, mamma frog had once been travelling. She had been sitting in the well's bucket one day when someone wound it up. But the sunlight had been too strong for her. It had given her a pain in the eyes, so she had leapt out of the bucket and plopped back into the water.

After that, the toads had not been bothered about finding out what the world was like. They just squatted in the well all day, wondering which one of them had a jewel in its head – for everyone knows the saying that ugly creatures can often hide precious gems inside. All except the youngest toad – who was also the ugliest.

"I know that I haven't got the jewel in my head," he said, shrugging his shoulders. "And I'm not bothered about it. All I want is to get up to the top of the well and take a peep. It must be wonderful out there!"

"Better stay where you are," said mamma toad, "it's dangerous!"

But the little toad felt a terrible longing to go and explore. The very next time the bucket began to be wound up, he hopped into it and was drawn up with it. Blinking in the daylight, he sprang out of the well with a great leap and went jumping into a clump of tall nettles.

"It's much lovelier here than down in the well," the little toad sighed, as he rested in the dappled

shade. "I could stay here all my life."

In fact, he lay there for two hours. Then he grew curious as to what else there was to see. He hopped away and came to a dry, dusty road. The little toad leapt across and was very glad when he reached a shady meadow on the other side. He hid among the beautiful flowers under the trees and watched a butterfly fluttering about. "How glorious to move about like that!" he sighed. "I wish I could too."

The little toad stayed there for almost a week. But then he found himself getting lonely, so off he hopped once again.

At length he came to a large pond with rushes around it. There he met a frog, who

invited him to a concert later that night. The toad enjoyed the music very much – but still he wanted to see more.

He hopped along, gazing up at the night sky. There were the stars twinkling, large and clear in the darkness. A full moon was shining, pale and bright. 'I wonder what those gleaming lights are,' the toad thought.

In the morning he reached a vegetable garden. "How green and pretty it is here," he murmured, and he rested there among some lettuce leaves, next to a friendly caterpillar.

In the house belonging to the garden lived two young men who were studying at college. One was a poet and one was a scientist. They came down the path through the garden and the scientist spotted the toad. "Look!" he cried excitedly. "I could use that toad for my experiments."

"You're always cutting up toads to look at their insides," said the poet, "you don't need another one – leave it alone."

So the two young men carried on along their way.

"Phew!" said the toad, breathing a sigh of relief. "That was a narrow escape."

"It was indeed," croaked a stork, high up on the rooftop. "Mind you, you could have leapt away and escaped. I can fly. Humans can only stagger about on two legs."

'My, this bird is a clever thinker,' thought the little toad, and settled down to listen. The

stork told the toad about everywhere she had been on her travels – especially about the warm land of Egypt, where she went to avoid the cold winters. It all sounded very exciting. "I must get to Egypt!" the little toad said to himself. "Maybe the stork will take me along one day? Yes, I'll get to Egypt,

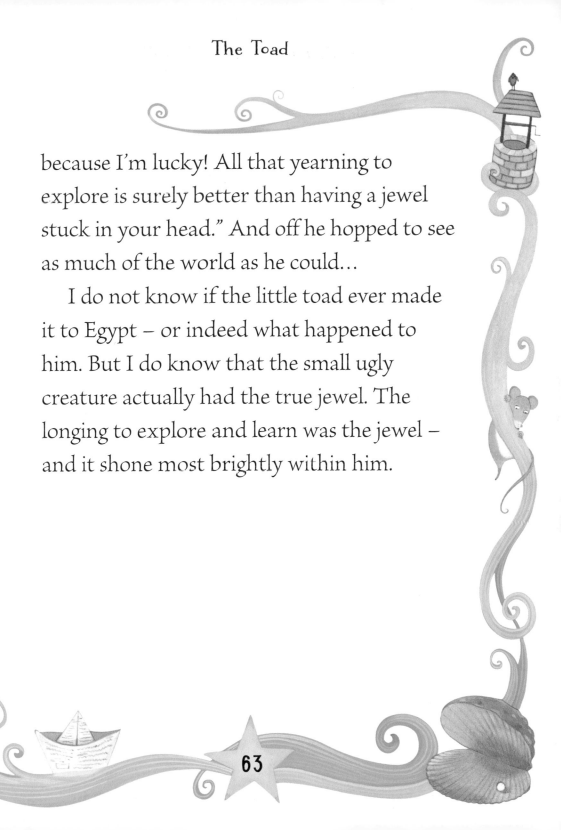

because I'm lucky! All that yearning to explore is surely better than having a jewel stuck in your head." And off he hopped to see as much of the world as he could...

I do not know if the little toad ever made it to Egypt – or indeed what happened to him. But I do know that the small ugly creature actually had the true jewel. The longing to explore and learn was the jewel – and it shone most brightly within him.

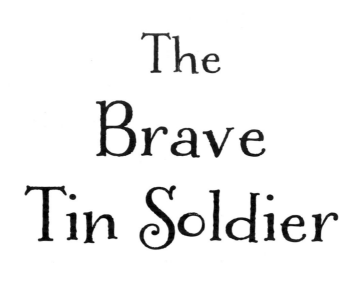

The
Brave
Tin Soldier

One Christmas, a little boy was given a dull-looking box as a present. But when he opened it, he was delighted. Inside were twenty-five tin soldiers. They wore smart red-and-blue uniforms and

looked straight ahead, shouldering their guns. They were brothers, because they had all been made out of the same old tin spoon. And they were all exactly alike except for one – he had only one leg, for he had been the last one to be made and there hadn't been enough tin to finish him off.

The little boy started playing with his new toys straight away. He arranged them on a table where there was a little cardboard castle. In front of the castle were model trees surrounding a piece of mirror for a lake, which had paper swans swimming on it.

At the open door of the castle stood a tiny lady. She was also a cardboard cut-out, but she wore a proper dress of floaty material, with a blue ribbon shawl around her shoulders, fixed in place with a glittering tinsel rose. The little lady was a dancer and she stretched out her arms and raised one leg so high that, from where the one-legged tin soldier was standing, he couldn't see it at all. He thought that she, like himself, had only one leg.

'That is the wife for me,' he thought. 'But she is grand and lives in a castle, while I have only a box to live in with my twenty-four brothers – that's no good for her.' Still, the one-legged tin soldier was determined to get to know her somehow.

When the little boy came down to play next morning, he lined up the tin soldiers

along the windowsill. But alas, the window was open. A gust of wind set a curtain fluttering, which caught the one-legged tin soldier and knocked him out. Down, down, down he fell, head over heel, and landed in the street below.

He lay there and was rained on. When the shower was over, two boys passed by and spotted him. They made a boat out of paper and placed the tin soldier in it, and sent him sailing down the gutter while they ran alongside, shouting with excitement. The paper boat rocked up and down, and sometimes span round so quickly that the tin soldier trembled. Yet he did not let his fear show – his face didn't flicker, he just looked

straight before him with his gun shouldered,
standing to attention.

Suddenly the boat shot into a drain and
then it was as dark as the tin soldier's box.
'Where am I going now?' he thought. 'If only
the little lady were here with me, I would not
mind the darkness.'

Out of the shadows a great water-rat
loomed. "Have you got a passport?" he
demanded. "Show it to me at once." But the
tin soldier remained silent and to attention,
holding his gun tighter than ever.

The boat sailed on in the gloom of the
tunnel, the strong current carrying it
forward. The rat followed it, gnashing his
teeth and shouting out, "Stop, you have not

shown your passport!"

All at once the soldier saw
the end of the drain approaching fast. Up
ahead, the stream became a waterfall, which
tumbled steeply down into a canal, back into
daylight. The poor tin soldier held himself as
stiffly as possible to show that he was not
afraid. His boat shot over the falls, filled with
water and began sinking in the canal. As the

water closed over his head, he thought of the beautiful little dancer whom he would never see again.

The soldier was quickly swallowed up by a fish. How dark it was! But still he stood firm. The fish swam to and fro for what seemed like days – then the tin soldier felt him become quite still. He waited… and waited… and finally daylight opened over him. A voice cried out, "I don't believe it, here is the missing tin soldier!"

The fish had been caught, taken to the market and sold to the little boy's mother, who took him home and cut him open to cook him for tea. She cleaned the soldier and carried him into the little boy's room. She put

him back on the table and there he was with his brothers again, back where he could gaze at the beautiful little dancer.

Unfortunately, the tin soldier didn't look the same after his adventures. The bright colours had been washed from his uniform. Later that day, the little boy picked him up and threw him onto the open fire in the hearth. The tin soldier lay there, still smartly to attention as the flames licked around him, his eyes fixed firmly on his beloved dancer.

Next morning, lying in the ashes of the fire, the boy's mother found a little tin heart.

The Snowdrop

It was wintertime. The air was cold and the wind was sharp, but under the snow where the flower-bulb lay it was warm and comfortable.

One day rain fell. The drops sank through

the snow into the earth. They touched the flower-bulb and talked of the bright world above. Soon a warm sunbeam pierced the snow and earth and tickled the root.

"I feel like stretching," yawned the flower-bulb. "It's time to get up."

Days passed and in the ground the bulb shot out a greenish-white bud on a stalk with thick, narrow leaves.

More sunbeams shone down to it. "Welcome!" they sang. "You are the first flower!" And the bud lifted itself up out of the snow into the brightness. The sunbeams kissed the bud and it opened with joy into a little white flower.

"How beautiful you are!" said the sunbeams, and the flower bent its head shyly. "Spring is coming and soon other flowers will bloom so you will have many friends."

But the wind howled and said: "You have arrived too early. Winter still rules. You should have stayed quietly at home and not come out to show yourself off. Your time has not yet come!"

All the next week, the wind blew thick clouds across the sky and there wasn't a single sunbeam. How cold it was! So cold that the little flower felt she might snap. Still, she stayed strong by thinking of the spring that the sunbeams had promised her would come.

"You silly thing, you'll break!" whispered

the snowflakes that came sweeping over her. "Why did you let yourself be tempted out of the earth?"

But some little children spotted her and cried out in delighted voices: "Oh look at the beautiful snowdrop! It's the very first flower to appear!"

These words warmed the flower and she was so joyful that she didn't even mind when a grown-up girl broke her off her stem, leaving just a little bit attached. The girl lay the flower in her hand and kissed her, then took her home and put her into a little vase of water in a warm room. The flower was thrilled. She thought spring had come at last!

One day, the girl wrote a poem about the

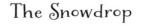

snowdrop – about how foolish it was to appear too soon, but how beautiful it was for being so brave, for daring to be the first flower and brightening up the bare winter days. She folded up the paper and slipped the flower inside. Then she popped it inside an envelope and posted it.

How dark it was for the snowdrop! But her journey soon came to an end when the letter was opened by the girl's sweetheart.

The young man was delighted. He read the poem over and over again, admiring the flower, then folded them back into the envelope and put it safely on a shelf.

The little flower lay there all through the spring… then summer passed by… the

autumn came and went… and winter arrived once again.

And then the young man became upset. One day he seized the envelope and threw it away, so that the flower fell out onto the ground. She was sad. She knew she had become very flat and faded, but she didn't think she deserved to be thrown on the ground. She didn't know that the young man's heart had been broken because his sweetheart had found another boy to love.

Next morning a cleaner came to sweep the room. She noticed the little flower on the floor, picked it up and laid it on an open storybook which was on the table. She thought that it must have been between the

pages and fallen out. She closed the book and tidied it away onto a bookshelf. There it stayed for years… until finally another young man took the book down from the shelf and began reading.

"Why, here's a flower!" he said, turning a page and finding the snowdrop.

"It must have been put in here for a special reason! I wonder what its story is…"

The little flower finally understood that everybody had been right all along. She had been both foolish and brave, all at the same time. And she was proud of it – that's what made her special.

The Silver Coin

Once upon a time, lots of coins were being made at a mint. One of them, a silver coin, came out very excited, shouting, "Hooray! Now I am going out into the wide world."

And so he did. He was used by many people to pay for things before he came to a man who was about to embark on travels to different countries. The traveller didn't realize that the silver coin was still in his pocket. When he found it, he thought it was a very nice surprise. "I'll keep it with me wherever I go, to remind me of home!" he decided, and he put it in his wallet.

Here the silver coin lay among lots of foreign coins. Some said they were French. Others said they were Italian. But none knew exactly where they were. The silver coin wished he could see out of the wallet, to get an idea of where he might be.

One day, he noticed that the wallet was

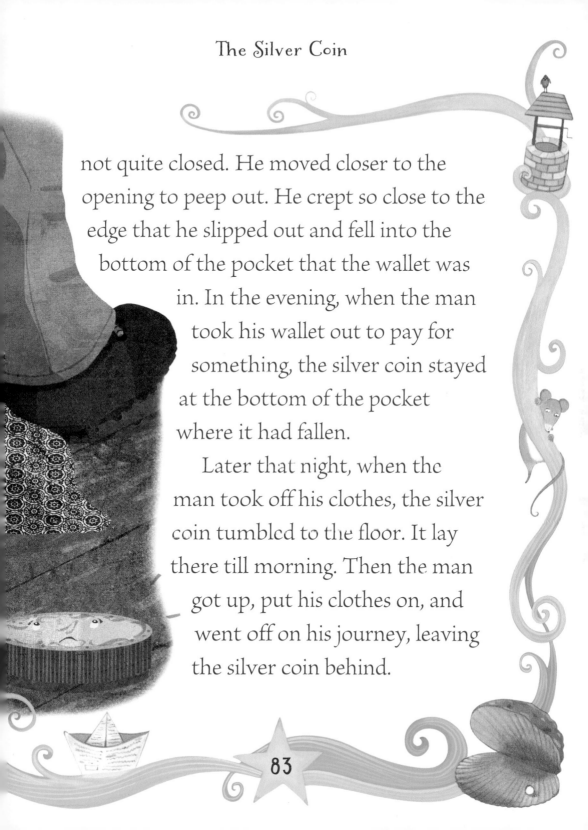

not quite closed. He moved closer to the opening to peep out. He crept so close to the edge that he slipped out and fell into the bottom of the pocket that the wallet was in. In the evening, when the man took his wallet out to pay for something, the silver coin stayed at the bottom of the pocket where it had fallen.

Later that night, when the man took off his clothes, the silver coin tumbled to the floor. It lay there till morning. Then the man got up, put his clothes on, and went off on his journey, leaving the silver coin behind.

The silver coin lay on the floor feeling sorry for himself until finally a woman found him. She didn't notice that he was from a strange country and put him straight into her purse. He found himself with three foreign coins, who were really nasty. "Call yourself money?" they sneered. "Whatever sort of coin are you? Are you just a pretend coin, like a toy that children play with?"

"Certainly not!" declared the silver coin.

But he soon found that he was, in fact, worthless. When the woman tried to use him to pay for something, the shopkeeper pointed out to her that he was a strange coin and wouldn't accept him. The poor silver coin realized that, so far from home, he couldn't

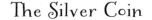

be used as money at all! This made him very sad as he began to believe that he was good for nothing…

The woman wondered what she was going to do with the coin, until a thought struck her. "Maybe you're a lucky coin," she said thoughtfully. "I know, I'll drill a hole through you and hang you on a pretty ribbon. Then I'll give you to my neighbour's little girl to wear as a lucky charm."

And that is exactly what she did. The silver coin didn't mind having a hole drilled through him, as he knew that it was for a good reason. He was hung on a ribbon and became a sort of medal. The neighbour's little girl loved her lucky necklace very much.

Unfortunately, the neighbour was a bad man. One night, he waited until his daughter was fast asleep and then cut the ribbon with scissors.

He took the coin and filled up the hole with cement, which he painted silver. Then he went out to a shop and handed over the coin to pay for a lottery ticket.

The silver coin never found out whether the lottery ticket had won the man any money or not – he very much hoped that it hadn't! But the next morning, the lottery ticket seller realized that he had a worthless coin among his money. He tutted at it in disgust and craftily passed it on to someone else who didn't notice...

And so the silver coin was sneered at and passed slyly from one dishonest hand to another. A whole year passed with nobody wanting him. It was a very lonely, sad time and the silver coin wondered whatever was to become of him.

But then one day he happened to be passed to the same traveller who had brought

him from home. A smile spread over his face and he said, "A coin from my own country. How strange that it's somehow come into my hands. It must be a lucky coin!"

From then on, the traveller looked after the silver coin very carefully. He wrapped him in tissue paper and kept him separate from his other money. When the traveller met people from his own country he showed them the silver

coin. Everyone admired the coin and spoke of him fondly.

At last, the traveller returned home – and the silver coin finally felt safe once more. He was back where he belonged, where he was useful and surrounded by friends. From then on, he told everyone he met that when times get tough, you should never give up hope – for if you stay strong and behave honestly, everything will turn out all right in the end.

Soup
from a
Sausage
Skewer

There was once a lady-mouse who
stood talking to another lady-mouse
about a splendid feast that had just been
held in the mouse-king's palace. "It was
wonderful! I wish you had been there," she

said to her friend. "I sat only twenty-one mice away from the mouse-king! We had fantastic food. There was stale bread for starters and wax candle for the main course. Pudding was the most delicious mouldy sausages. In the end there wasn't anything left except the skewers that the sausages had been stuck on for grilling. Then everyone started talking about the old recipe, soup made from sausage skewers.

"We had all heard of the soup, but no one had actually ever tasted it or made it themselves. Then the mouse-king stood up – and guess what he promised? He said that the lady-mouse who could make the tastiest soup from a sausage skewer would be his

bride. He would give us a year and a day to find out the recipe and practise making it."

"Ooooh!" gasped the second lady-mouse. "How exciting!"

"Well, of course everyone wants to be his bride," said the first mouse, "but in the end only four lady-mice had the courage to say they would go out into the world to search for the recipe. We will have to wait and see how they get on…"

A year and a day later, the mouse-king ordered everyone to gather in his palace kitchen. A great crowd arrived – to find that only three of the brave lady-mice who had been travelling were there. Nobody knew what had happened to the fourth. Everyone

stood in silence, waiting excitedly, and then
the king beckoned the first lady-mouse
traveller forward. "Tell me your story,"
he ordered.

"I boarded a ship, for I thought that the
cook must have travelled to many far-off
countries and learned about strange recipes,"
she squeaked. "But he knew nothing of how
to make soup from a sausage skewer.

"We sailed to a strange land and I went
ashore and asked all the creatures I came
across. No one had heard of the recipe. I even
met some elves, but they didn't know either,"
the little mouse sighed. "Although they
showed me how to do this…" She held up her
sausage skewer, touched the mouse-king with

it, and it blossomed with beautiful violets, one after another. She waved it as though she were conducting music and suddenly the sound of cooking arose – pots simmered, pans bubbled, kettles whistled – and all sorts of tasty smells filled the air.

"That is as far as I got with my soup," she finished sadly.

"If that is all," said the mouse-king disappointedly, "let's hear from the next lady-mouse."

"My family live in a library," she began. "We nibble away at all the books and so we are extremely clever. My old grandma was sure that in one of the books was written: 'Anyone who can make soup out of a sausage skewer is a poet.' I asked her what I needed to do to become a poet. My grandma said that poets need to be clever, and to have a big imagination and plenty of feeling.

"I thought I could find all that in the library books. So I read my way through everything. I learned so much that I am sure I became clever. My imagination grew enormous. I read so many stories that I felt every feeling under the sun. At last, I was certain that I must be a poet. I thought over everything I knew about sausages and skewers and soup – and I wrote a long poem about it. And that is my soup."

"In that case," said the mouse-king, "we will hear what the third mouse has to say."

"Squeak, squeak," cried a little mouse dashing in at the kitchen door – it was the fourth traveller! "I am sorry I am late," she interrupted, quite out of breath. "I travelled far away on a train and ended up in a prison. There were hundreds of men there but none knew how to make soup from a sausage skewer. The prison warder caught me and trapped me in a cage where I had to run in a wheel, round and round all day. I was there so long I thought I would never get out again! But one day the prison warder's daughter took pity on me and freed me.

"I scampered away from the prison and came to a high tower. A wise owl lived there, and so I peeped from a safe hole in the wall and asked if she knew how to make soup from a sausage skewer. I must say, the answer surprised me.

"She told me it is not a real recipe at all, just a human saying. She said it means 'make something out of nothing'. I thought about this for a long time and finally decided that it must be the truth. So this is what I bring you – not soup, but the truth."

Then the third lady-mouse piped up. "That is all wrong!" she said. "I can prepare the soup – and I will do it now."

"Please do," said the king, very curious.

"I did not travel," said the third mouse. "I did not get my knowledge from elves, nor books, nor owls. I have got it all from simply

thinking and using my head.

"Now, will someone set the kettle on the fire? Pour the water in – quite full, right up to the brim… now we wait until the water comes to the boil… there, I throw in my sausage skewer… and now will the mouse-king be pleased to dip his tail into the boiling water and stir it round? The longer the king stirs it, the stronger the soup will become. Nothing more is needed, only to stir it."

"Can't anyone else do this?" asked the mouse-king nervously, looking at the bubbling, steaming water.

"No," said the third lady-mouse firmly. "The power is contained in your tail only, and no one else's."

So the mouse-king stood close beside the kettle and carefully put out his tail – closer, closer, closer… It had only just touched the hot steam when he sprang away from it,

exclaiming, "Oh, certainly, by all means, you must be my queen! And the soup is so special that we won't make it now, we will save it for our fiftieth anniversary and have it then at a feast for everyone."

Very soon the wedding took place. But many of the mice, as they were returning home, said that the soup could not be properly called 'soup from a sausage skewer', but 'soup from a mouse's tail'.

What do you think?

The Thistle's Tale

Long ago and far away, there was a rich family who lived in a grand manor house. The house had a huge, beautiful garden, filled with flowers and trees. The family made sure that the garden was always carefully looked after. They were very proud of it, and people often asked permission to come and wander round, to admire and enjoy it.

Just outside the garden, by the fence at the roadside, grew a huge thistle. It spread out in all directions and was more of a bush than a single plant. Nobody took any notice of it, except the old donkey which drew the milkmaid's cart. He thought it looked very tasty! When he was tied up at the roadside he would stretch out his head towards the thistle and say, "You are so beautiful, I would like to eat you!" But try as he might, he could never quite reach it.

There came a time when the family at the

manor house had visitors from abroad. Several young men and women from different places were staying with them, including one young lady from a country called Scotland. She was the loveliest of the girls and all the boys wanted the chance to get to know her.

For two days, the family and their guests all enjoyed themselves in the garden. They had lunch on the patio, they played games on the lawn, and they wandered around enjoying the flowers. Each of the girls broke off a flower, chose a young man and threaded it into their buttonhole – except for the girl from Scotland. She looked at the flowers for a long time. She thought they were all very beautiful, but none of them would do.

Then her eye fell outside the fence, to the great thistle bush. She saw its strong, spiky purple flowers and smiled. She asked the son of the house to pick one for her. "It is my country's flower," she said, "the flower of Scotland." The young man picked the best thistle flower for her and she threaded it carefully through his buttonhole.

The young man was highly delighted – and the thistle bush was too. "I must be something very special!" he said to himself. "I suppose that I should really be inside the garden, not outside the fence. Well, I've managed to get one of my lovely flowers inside, at least!"

A few days went by and then a little bird told the thistle bush that the lovely Scottish girl had agreed to marry the son of the house. "And all because of me!" exclaimed the thistle bush. "Now surely someone will dig me up, take me into the garden and replant me there. Maybe they will put me in a pot, in pride of place. I know that is meant to be a very great honour!"

But nothing like that came to pass. Instead, the thistle bush just stood there… and stood there… and stood there.

"I am expecting any moment to be taken across the fence," he explained to a few daisies and a long, thin dandelion. "I am the national flower of Scotland, you know. I must come from a very grand family." The little wildflowers were very impressed by the thistle bush and believed everything it said.

The summer went by… and the autumn. The leaves fell from the trees and the few flowers which were left had deeper colours and less perfume. Young fir trees in the forest began to long for Christmas.

"I am standing here still!" exclaimed the

thistle bush. "It seems as if everyone's forgotten about me – and yet, I am the reason that the young lady and the young man fell in love."

A few more weeks went by and the thistle still stood there, with just one last flower remaining on it.

Then the young pair, now man and wife, came into the garden. "There's the great thistle still growing," the lady said, looking across the fence. "Look – it has one last flower on it."

So the young man went outside the fence, picked the flower, and off they went with it into the house.

"My, my!" exclaimed the thistle bush. "My

first child was put into a buttonhole, and my last-born child has been taken into the house. They were very important, so surely I'm

going to be put somewhere special now –
I wonder where…"

The milkmaid's donkey was tied up by
the roadside. "Come to me, my darling," he
said, "and I will eat you! I can't reach you
from here."

But the thistle took no notice. A thought
had suddenly struck him. He pondered for a
good long while and then announced:
"Maybe if you are a parent, and good things
happen to your children, perhaps you
shouldn't mind if good things don't happen
to you too."

"That's an honourable thought," replied a
sunbeam. "And for that, you truly do deserve
a good place."

"In a buttonhole, in a pot, or in the house?" asked the thistle.

"In a story, of course!" said the sunbeam.

LOOKING AND SEEING

The Jumpers

Once upon a time, a flea, a grasshopper and a goose wanted to see which one could jump the highest. They decided to hold a festival where they would have a jumping competition against each

other. They invited the whole world – and a few others – to watch, and everyone met together in a big room, very excited.

"What's the prize?" asked the king.

The flea looked at the grasshopper, and the grasshopper looked at the goose, and the goose looked back at the flea. "There isn't one," they all said together.

"Well, it seems a bit mean to have you all jumping for nothing," said the king. "I'll tell you what – I'll give my daughter to the one who jumps the highest." Everyone cheered and clapped and thought that was an excellent idea.

Then a clever monkey started the competition by doing the introductions.

"Ladies and gentlemen!"
he roared. "He may be small
in size but he's big in determination! Please
put your hands together for...THE FLEA!"

The flea had beautiful manners and
bowed right and left. "I come from a noble
family," he announced. "Our motto is: Never
give up!" Everyone cheered and clapped
some more.

The grasshopper was next. "Ladies and gentlemen!" the monkey bellowed. "He's lean, he's green – he's a lean green jumping machine! Give a very warm welcome to… THE GRASSHOPPER!"

The grasshopper was bigger and heavier than the flea, but he was equally well mannered. "I come from Egypt, where my family are very famous singers," he declared proudly. Everyone oohed and aahed and was suitably impressed.

"Surely both the flea and the grasshopper are good enough to marry the princess," a little boy in the crowd said.

Then the monkey announced the last contestant. "He's a goose – and he jumps,"

he bellowed. "Heeeeeeeeeeeere's… THE JUMPING GOOSE!" And everyone cheered and clapped all over again.

The goose said nothing at all, but everyone decided that that meant he must be thinking a lot. The king's dog went over and sniffed at him. "Oh yes, he definitely comes from a very good family," he remarked gruffly.

"Good-o," said the king.

And then it was time for the competition.

The flea jumped first – and he went so high that nobody could see him. So everyone said he hadn't jumped at all, but had only been pretending!

The grasshopper only jumped half as high as the flea – but he jumped right into the

king's face! "Eeurrrrgh!" spat the king, shocked and disgusted.

The goose stood still for a long time, lost in thought, and people began to wonder if he could jump at all.

"I hope he isn't ill," said the court dog, and gave him another sniff. Then suddenly – *PLOP!* The goose jumped sideways, straight into the lap of the princess, who was sitting on a little golden stool.

"Splendid!" cried the king. "To jump up to my daughter is the highest jump that can be made.

It takes brains to get an idea like that – and the goose has shown that he does have brains. He is a very clever fellow."

So the jumping goose won the princess.

"I don't care a bit," said the flea. "I jumped the highest." And he went to join the circus.

"I don't care either," said the grasshopper. "I'm still the best singer." And he went back to Egypt to star in concerts with his family.

And so the jumping goose married the princess and they lived happily ever after. Although the whole story may just be rumours and gossip…

The Snow Queen

Long ago, there was a very wicked sprite. For fun, he made a magic mirror. In it, anything that was good and beautiful had an evil, ugly reflection. The sprite ran about with the mirror, laughing at how horrible he could make people and places look. But suddenly the mirror slipped out of his hands. It smashed into a billion pieces, tinier than grains of sand. The wind blew them all over the world...

A little boy called Kay was looking at a picture book with his friend from next door, Gerda, when suddenly he cried out: "Oh, I've got something in my eye!" He blinked and winked, and the little girl checked his eye but couldn't see anything. "I think it is out now," Kay said, but it wasn't. He had got one of the pieces from the magic mirror stuck in his eye. Little did Kay know, anything beautiful now appeared ugly to him...

Very quickly, Kay became bitter and cruel.

He no longer wanted to play with Gerda, and teased her nastily when she got upset.

One day, thick snow began to fall. Gerda looked out of her window and saw Kay with the other boys from their street, carrying their sledges. They were off to play in the marketplace. There the boys took turns tying their sledges on to the back of horse-drawn carts, so they would be pulled along and get a good ride.

No one except Kay seemed to notice a large, horse-drawn sleigh glide into the square. The sleigh was a gleaming white and the driver was a woman all wrapped up in a white fur cloak and cap. Kay did not know it, but she was the wicked Snow Queen. "Come

and warm up in my sleigh," she coaxed. Kay
looked back at the other boys, but they were
all busy playing – it was as if they couldn't see
him or the fine sleigh and the beautiful lady.
Turning away from them, Kay climbed in.
The Snow Queen wrapped her fur cloak
around him and kissed his forehead – and
with that magic kiss Kay quite forgot his
home, his family and his little friend, Gerda.

The Snow Queen cracked the whip and
they were off like the wind, into the whirling
snowflakes. The sleigh lifted and Kay realized
they were flying, not sliding. On they rushed,
through the icy air, all the way to the far
north and the Snow Queen's palace. There
Kay stayed with the Snow Queen, under her

wicked spell, having forgotten everything he had once known…

How worried everyone was, when Kay didn't come back! Nobody had any idea what had happened to him. Days went by, and turned into weeks, which turned into months… Finally Kay's family sadly decided that he must have fallen into the river and drowned.

But his little friend Gerda didn't believe it. Early one morning she thought, 'I'll go and ask the river myself.' Off she went to the riverbank, and cried out, "Is it true that you have taken my friend? If you have, give him back!" It seemed as though the blue waves were nodding and beckoning to her. So Gerda

stepped into a boat which lay among the rushes, untied the rope, and let it drift out into the current. 'Perhaps the river will carry me to Kay,' she thought, and she tried not to be frightened.

The boat swept out of the town and through the countryside until the sun was high in the sky. Then it bumped into the riverbank right by a little cottage. An old woman came out and helped Gerda on to dry land. Gerda asked if the old woman had seen or heard of Kay. "I haven't, my dear," the old woman replied. "But do go and ask the flowers in my garden. You never know, they may know something."

Gerda wandered around the cottage

garden, asking the daisies, the tulips and the roses if they had seen Kay. Sadly, they all shook their heads.

When Gerda came to the far end of the garden, she found a little rusty gate. She shook the bolt loose, then pushed the gate open and stepped through. To her surprise, she discovered that the whole summer had passed. Outside the gate, the leaves on the trees were yellow and orange and red – it was now autumn.

As Gerda stood in astonishment, some nearby wood-pigeons called out, "Coo! Coo! We have seen little Kay! He was sitting in the sleigh of the Snow Queen. They were no doubt on their way to her palace in Lapland."

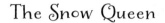

"Which way should I go?" cried the brave little girl.

"Ask the reindeer over there," cooed the wood-pigeons.

Gerda looked and saw a stately reindeer standing at the edge of a forest. "Do you know where the Snow Queen's palace is, in Lapland?" she asked.

"Of course I do," said the animal. "I was born and bred in Lapland. Jump on my back and I will take you."

So Gerda clambered on, held tight to his mighty antlers, and off they flew, through the forest and over snowy mountains, until they arrived in Lapland.

The reindeer took Gerda right up to the

Snow Queen's glittering frost palace. She slipped off the reindeer's back, so chilled that she could barely speak to say thank you.

Determined to be brave, Gerda crept into the palace. She found herself in an empty, endless, snowy hall. And there before her sat little Kay. He was all alone, for the Snow Queen had flown away on her sleigh to spread winter around the world.

Gerda ran to Kay in joy. But to her horror, he was quite blue with cold. He didn't realize it at all, for he was under the Snow Queen's spell. He just sat there, making patterns in the snow with an icicle.

"Kay!" Gerda whispered, putting her

arm around him gently. "Don't you remember me?" Still Kay sat, numb and motionless with cold.

Then Gerda began to cry. Her warm tears fell on Kay and melted away the Snow Queen's icy kiss. Kay slowly began to remember his little friend and his family, and he burst into tears too. "Gerda! Where have you been for so long? And where am I? Why is it so cold?" Kay wept so much that the splinter of mirror in his eye was washed out.

"The Snow Queen took you prisoner," Gerda explained. "Now, quick, we must escape before she comes back."

Hand in hand they ran out of the vast hall, jumped on the faithful reindeer's back and were off, over snowy mountains and meadows, all the way back to the gates of their town.

As the reindeer trotted away, the children took each other's hand. They turned to look at each other – and realized they were grown up. From that moment on, they only ever remembered the Snow Queen as though they had been dreaming…

The Darning Needle

Once upon a time, there lived a darning needle. She was big and thick, and people used her to mend holes in old socks and vests. However, she thought very highly of herself and saw herself as something special. She imagined she was so delicate and fine that she was really a sewing needle, which people used to carefully embroider clever pictures and pretty patterns in coloured thread.

"Be careful and hold me tightly!" she warned the fingers that picked her up. They belonged to the cook. "Don't drop me!" cried the darning needle. "If you do, you may never find me again – that's how fine I am!"

"That's what you think!" said the fingers, and squeezed her around her thick waist.

"Look, here I come – like a princess with a beautiful train!" said the darning needle, as the cook threaded a long piece of wool through her.

The Darning Needle

The cook aimed the needle
straight at a smelly leather slipper,
which had a hole that needed to be mended.

"My! What a horrible job!" sniffed the
darning needle. "That old slipper's whiffy –
and the leather's so tough I'll never get
through! Look out! I'm breaking! I'm
breaking in two." And just then the point of

the needle did break off. "I told you so," she
said. "I'm much too delicate!"

"Well, that needle will never darn
anything again," said the cook to herself.
She took the broken needle and used it to
pin the ends of her shawl together around
her shoulders.

"Look! Now I'm a brooch!" said the needle.
"I knew I was important." She sat on the
cook's chest and looked all around, very
pleased with herself. The darning needle
drew herself up so proudly that when the
cook began rinsing out the sink, she fell right
out of the shawl and into the basin.

"It looks now as if I am off on an
adventure," she said to herself happily.

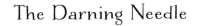

"I wonder where I might be going…"

The darning needle was washed down the drain and fell into the gutter outside, where she got stuck with her broken end wedged into a crack.

"I'm too fine for this world," she thought calmly. She lay there, still proud, as many strange things washed past her – rubbish and twigs and bits of old newspapers. "Look at them sail past, thinking only of themselves!" she said to herself. "They don't know who I am! But I do – and I shall never forget it."

Next day, the darning needle saw something beside her that glittered splendidly in the sunlight. It was only a bit of a broken bottle, but because the darning needle was

137

quite sure it was something valuable, like a
diamond, she spoke to it.

"I am a beautiful brooch," the
darning needle said, "and I suppose
you're a diamond?"

"Something like that," came the reply.
But just then a stream of water
came rushing down the gutter and the
bit of broken bottle was
washed away.

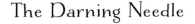

"What a shame," remarked the darning needle, "that sparkling jewel would have been suitable company for me. But never mind…" And she sat up straight, lost in many big thoughts of herself.

The following day some street boys came searching around in the gutter, looking for lost money. It was filthy work, but they didn't mind – they just wanted to find a coin or two.

"Look at this!" one cried as he spotted the darning needle. "You're an interesting fellow," he said as he picked her out of the crack.

"I'm not a fellow, I'm a young lady," replied the darning needle stuffily, although of course they couldn't hear her.

"Look!" cried the boys. "Here comes an eggshell sailing along." They stuck the darning needle fast into the shell like a mast in a boat.

"Wonderful! People can really see me now," cried the darning needle.

But at that very moment – *CRACK!* went the eggshell, for a bicycle ran over it. The darning needle was shattered into tiny pieces, before she had ever got to really see herself.

The
Drop
of
Water

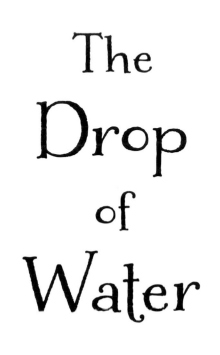

Once there was an old man called
Cribble-Crabble. He was a curious sort
of person and liked doing scientific
experiments to find things out – but he
enjoyed dabbling in magic too. His home was

filled with strange equipment – small glass tubes, wooden mixing bowls, iron cauldrons... although his most prized possession was his microscope.

You know what a microscope is – a little tube that you look through to see tiny things made thousands of times bigger. Through a microscope, you can see all sorts of things quite clearly that don't seem to be there at all if you just look with your eyes.

Cribble-Crabble was always so amazed by his microscope that he could never decide whether it was just scientific equipment or whether there was something magic about it after all...

One day, Cribble-Crabble was out walking

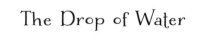

when he came across a muddy puddle. This gave him an idea. He scooped up a little of the water into a flask and took it home with him. There, he carefully put one drop of the water onto a thin sliver of glass. He fixed the glass slide at the bottom of the microscope. Then Cribble-Crabble shut one eye, and with the

143

"What have you got there?" asked the neighbour, who was also a magician.

"See if you can guess," replied Cribble-Crabble mysteriously.

So the second magician peered down through the microscope. He almost jumped back in alarm as he saw all the tiny beings kicking and punching, and struggling to clamber on top of one another.

"Oh my goodness, it's a tiny city!" gasped the second magician. "You've conjured up a tiny city full of strange angry creatures!"

"No!" cried Cribble-Crabble, triumphantly. "It's a drop of muddy water."

The second magician thought hard, but he couldn't decide whether the microscope was science or magic either.

What do you think?

The Butterfly

There was once a butterfly who wanted to fall in love. He didn't want a lady butterfly for a wife, he wanted to marry one of the flowers. The only problem was, he couldn't decide which was the prettiest. He flew around looking at them all, sitting quietly on their stalks – there were so many that he thought it would be quite impossible to decide!

The butterfly had an idea. He remembered that daisies can tell people's fortunes – he had once seen a young man picking off a daisy's petals saying, "She loves me... she loves me not... she loves me... she loves me not..." So he flew down to a pretty daisy and said: "Sweet Miss Daisy – you're the wisest of all the flowers. Please tell me which flower I should choose – this one or that one? As soon as you've told me, I will fly straight to her and ask her to marry me."

But the daisy didn't say a thing. She didn't

think any of the flowers would want to marry a butterfly!

The butterfly asked for a second time... and a third time... but the daisy still refused to speak to him, so eventually he gave up and flew away.

It was early spring and there were hundreds of little snowdrops and crocuses about. "They're really very charming," said the butterfly, "but they're all a bit too young for me."

He flew to the violets, but he thought their scent was too strong.

He flew to the tulips, but soon decided that their bright colours were just too showy for him.

Next, he flew to the apple blossoms. The butterfly thought they were almost as beautiful as roses. But he knew that if they opened on a windy day, a gust would blow them to pieces. "I want my marriage to last," he said to himself.

Then the butterfly noticed the sweet peas. He fluttered over and his eyes fell on one that he thought was most beautiful of all – she was red and white and dainty and delicate. 'That's the flower for me,' he decided. He was just about to ask her to marry him when he noticed a pea pod hanging nearby with a withered, dried-up, crinkled old flower clinging to it.

"Who's that?" he asked.

The Butterfly

"It's my sister," said the sweet pea flower.

"Oh, so that's how you'll look when you are older!" gasped the butterfly, in horror. He was quite put off and flew away as quickly as he could.

Spring passed… and summer passed… then autumn came, and the butterfly was still no nearer making up his mind. Whenever he looked at all the flowers in their long, colourful dresses, he got so confused that he just couldn't decide.

The weather became windy and wet, and very cold. One day the butterfly came across a room where there was a crackling fire in the stove and the air was as warm as summer. He flew in through the window and fluttered

about. The people in the room were charmed
by his pretty colours. They caught him and
pinned him to a piece of cardboard, then set
him in a big glass frame so everyone could
look at him and admire him for ever.

The Butterfly

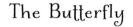

"Now I'm sitting on a stalk, just like the flowers," the butterfly sighed. "And I must admit, it isn't very much fun." Too late, he realized he had been looking at things wrongly all along. "Beauty just isn't enough to make you happy," he sighed. "To be happy, you must have freedom and sunshine."

And although the butterfly never did find a wife, he was comforted by his own reflection in the glass frame, which kept him company.

The Ugly Duckling

It was summer and it was beautiful in the countryside. In the golden wheat fields lay an old manor house with a deep moat around it. The bank at the edge of the moat was thick with reeds, and there sat a duck on her nest, hatching her ducklings. She had been sitting there a long time and was getting rather fed up with it. But at last the eggshells began to crack, one after another. "Peep, peep!" said the little ducklings, as they poked out their heads.

"Quack, quack!" said the mother duck, and the ducklings all clambered out of the nest to explore. "I do hope you are all hatched," she said, as she checked her nest. "Oh dear, there's one egg left – and it's the biggest one! I wonder how much longer this is going to take…" and she settled back down. "I'll sit a little longer," she murmured. "I've been at it so long already that I suppose a bit longer won't make any difference."

A few days later, the big egg did at last crack. "Peep," said the young one, and out he tumbled. To the mother duck's surprise, he wasn't at all like the other ducklings!

"Oooh, that's a frightfully big, ugly, grey duckling!" the duck said to herself. "He doesn't look at all like the others. They're all small and pretty, and look just like their father. But this one – my goodness! Never mind, he's mine, so I shall treat him just the same as the rest…"

Next day, the mother duck led her whole
family into the moat. *Splash!* She plopped into
the water. "Quack, quack," she said, and one
duckling after another plunged in after her.
The water went over their heads, but they
came up in a flash, floating perfectly. Their
legs started paddling away and there they all
were, swimming along. Even the big, ugly
grey one was doing well.

"Quack, quack! Follow me," the mother
duck called, and off she went, leading them
down the moat a little way before hopping
out into the duck yard.

What a commotion was going on! All the
other ducks were there, fighting over food.
The plump, grown-up birds ran around the

little ducklings, grumbling, "Oh no! Must we have this lot too! There's too many of us already… And whoever's that ugly-looking thing? We don't want him around here."

Suddenly a nasty duck charged up and bit the ugly grey duckling's neck.

"Leave him alone," scolded the mother duck. "He isn't doing any harm."

"Maybe not," hissed the nasty duck, "but he's too big and strange, he shouldn't be round here with us…"

Every day it was the same. The poor ugly duckling who had been the last one out of his egg was pecked and pushed about and made fun of by all the other ducks – and the chickens too. "He's too big – and so ugly!"

they clucked. The turkey tried to chase him away, gobbling till he was red in the face. Even his own brothers and sisters began to be nasty to him. "We wish the cat would catch you, you ugly thing!" they sneered. And meanwhile his mother just sighed and said, "Oh dear, you always seem to cause trouble wherever you go..."

The poor duckling was the laughing stock of the whole farmyard. He was so sad...

So he ran away.

One day, he just sprang up into the air and flew over the fence. The little birds in the bushes darted up in fright. 'That's because I'm so ugly,' he thought sadly. Then he ran as hard as he could until he reached the marsh

where all the wild ducks lived.

"What sort of creature are you?" the wild ducks asked. "You are terribly ugly," they told him, "but we will let you stay round here – as long as you keep your distance!"

So there the ugly duckling stayed. The other ducks allowed him to swim on the water and dive down in it for food, but they all kept away because he was so ugly. No one spoke to him. No one cared about him. Poor duckling! How alone he was!

Weeks went by and autumn arrived. The leaves in the forest turned yellow and brown, and the wind caught them and whirled them about until they fell to the ground.

One evening, just as the sun was setting in

a blaze of red and gold, a great flock of large, handsome birds appeared out of the reeds.

The duckling had never seen birds so beautiful. They were dazzling white, with long graceful necks – they were swans. Stretching out their wings, they uttered a strange cry and then soared up into the sky, flying away to warmer countries for the winter.

As the duckling watched them, a strange feeling came over him. He craned his neck to watch where they went and his heart began to ache. Oh, how he longed to be with those wonderful birds!

Winter soon came and the weather grew cold – so cold that the marsh became icy and the duckling nearly froze to death. Every day, he kept himself going with the thought of seeing those magnificent birds once again.

At last, when the warm sun of springtime finally shone, the duckling was still alive among the reeds.

One morning, quite suddenly, the duckling spread his wings wide. With a few swishes, he was off into the air. His wings seemed to sweep him through the air much more strongly than before and their powerful strokes carried him far. Before the duckling quite knew what was happening, he found himself landing in a winding stream through a beautiful garden – and three lovely white swans were swimming towards him.

The ugly duckling bowed his head before
the noble birds, waiting for them to peck at
him and call him names and chase him away.
But what did he see, as he looked down at the
water? His reflection was no longer a grey,
ugly bird. He was a *swan!*

The Ugly Duckling

The three great swans came swimming around him and stroked him with their bills. Then several little children came into the garden to throw grain and bits of bread upon the water. "Look, there's a new one!" the smallest child cried. "Yes, and he's the most handsome of all," the others agreed.

The young swan rustled his feathers, held his neck high, and cried out: "I never dreamed that I could be so happy, when I was the ugly duckling!"

The Beetle

The emperor's horse was a magnificent animal, with intelligent eyes and a mane like silk. He had carried his master through the smoke and flame of battle, saving his life. And so the emperor ordered the royal blacksmith to make him four horseshoes out of pure gold – one for each hoof.

As the blacksmith banged away in the stable, he was most surprised to see a tiny beetle come creeping out to talk to him.

"I want golden shoes too!" squeaked the little beetle.

"You must be crazy!" said the blacksmith. "Why on earth do you want golden shoes?"

"Well," said the beetle, "I'm just as good as that great creature that is waited on, and groomed, and served with food and drink. I live here in the royal stable, so don't I belong to the emperor too?"

"But do you know *why* the horse is getting

golden shoes?" asked the blacksmith. "Don't you understand that?"

"I understand that it's being done just to annoy me," said the beetle.

"Get out of here!" ordered the blacksmith.

So the beetle left the stable, mumbling, "What a rude person!" He flew a little way and presently found himself in a beautiful flower garden.

"Isn't it lovely here?" asked one of the little ladybirds that were flying about. "How sweet it smells and how beautiful it is!"

"I'm used to much better things," said the beetle. "Do you call *this* beautiful? Why, there isn't even a manure pile here!" and he crawled into the shadow of a big wallflower.

The Beetle

"How beautiful the world is," said a caterpillar, who was sheltering there. "The sun is so warm, and everything is so pleasant, and one day I'll have wings and be a beautiful butterfly!"

"How dare you!" said the beetle. "*You* fly about like a butterfly, indeed! I'm from the stable of the emperor, and no one there, not even the emperor's favourite horse, has any grand ideas like that. Get wings! Fly! Why, I can fly already!" And the beetle flew off.

Soon afterwards he settled on a large lawn. Here he lay quietly for a while, and then he fell asleep.

All at once, the rain began to pour down. The beetle woke up and wanted to dig down

into the earth, but he couldn't.
He tumbled over and over;
sometimes he was
swimming on his
stomach, sometimes on
his back, and it was out of
the question to try to fly.

When the rain had let up a
little, and the beetle had blinked the
water from his eyes, he saw that he
had been washed up near two frogs
sitting on a stone.

"What wonderful weather this is!" one
of them said.

"Yes, how refreshing!" agreed the other.
"Have you ever been in the emperor's

stable?" asked the beetle. "The dampness there is both warm and refreshing. That's what I am used to – that's the weather for me. Now is there a warm spot here in the garden where someone important like me can dry themselves off?"

But the frogs either couldn't or wouldn't understand him.

"I never ask a question twice," said the beetle, after he had repeated himself three times without getting any answer. So off he crawled.

As the beetle travelled on through the garden, the sun warmed and dried his wings. He shook them, gave a little wriggle, then jumped up into the air and sailed away on the breeze – all the way through the open window of a greenhouse. There, he buried himself in some warm compost in a plant pot to rest.

"It's very comfortable here," he remarked.

The beetle fell asleep and had a wonderful dream. He dreamed that the emperor's horse had fallen down and hurt his leg, so that he was no longer any use. Then he, Mr Beetle, had been given the golden shoes, with the promise that he should have two more.

When the beetle woke up, he crept out of the compost and flew away – all the way back to the royal stable. To his dismay, he saw that the emperor's horse was quite fit and well, with his golden shoes gleaming.

The Beetle

The beetle sank down on the horse's long, fine, soft mane, very disappointed – and then a thought struck him.

"Well, here I am sitting on the emperor's favourite horse!" he said to himself. "Yes, sitting on him as his rider. Now it's quite clear to me – yes, it's a good idea and I'm sure it's right – the horse was given golden shoes *because of me*! Because I'm his rider and that's what I deserve – a horse with golden shoes!"

The beetle was quite cheered up again. "I've always heard it said that travelling broadens your mind and helps you to see things more clearly," he said. And to the beetle, the world was wonderful, because the emperor's favourite horse had golden shoes and because he was his rider.

The Snowman

"How delightfully cold it is!" said the snowman. "I feel as though my body is crackling all over. But how that fiery thing up there glares!" He meant the sun, which was just setting.

Some young boys had had great fun making him. For eyes, the snowman had two large flat grey pebbles. And his mouth was the end of an old rake, so it looked like he actually had teeth!

The snowman stood, unblinking, as the sun went down. Then the moon rose, large, round, clear and beautiful in the dark blue sky. "Here it comes again," said the snowman, thinking that the moon was actually the sun coming back. "I am getting quite used to it now. I hope it will hang there and shine so that it gets light again and I might be able to see myself. I would love to know what I look like! I'd love even more to be able to move about and glide up and down on the ice as gracefully as I saw those boys doing earlier on!"

"Woof!" barked a dog, who was out in a nearby garden. "The sun will soon teach you to run. I saw that last year, with the snowman that the boys built then – and the same with the one they made the year before. All snowmen end up running away!"

"I don't understand you," said the

snowman. "Do you mean that thing up there will teach me how to run?"

"You know nothing at all," said the dog, sniffing. "That thing up there is the moon. The other thing you saw earlier was the sun. He will come back again tomorrow and will soon teach you how to run – run away down the gutter."

"I still don't understand," the snowman muttered to himself, "but I think he must mean that something nasty is going to happen. I have a feeling that the sun, as he calls it, is not my friend."

"Woof! Woof!" barked the dog. Then he trotted back indoors to sleep.

Next morning, the sun rose over a glorious

sight. Everything was covered with frost. The trees and shrubs and grass were glistening white, and everything glittered as if it had been sprinkled with diamond dust.

"Isn't it wonderful?" exclaimed a girl who came walking along with a young man. They stopped near the snowman to look at the glistening trees. "Even summer isn't as beautiful as this," she said, her eyes shining.

"And you can't make a splendid fellow like this in summer, either," said the young man, pointing to the snowman. "He's a beauty!" They both smiled and patted the snowman, then crunched away.

"Who were they?" the snowman asked the dog, who was back outside in the garden again. "Do you know who they are?"

"Do I know them?" answered the dog. "She has often stroked me, and he gives me bones!"

"But what are they?" asked the snowman with great curiosity.

"They are our masters," answered the dog. "Really, creatures who have only been in the world one day know very little!"

"Tell me some more," begged the snowman. "Please!"

"All right then," agreed the dog, quite happy to make more noise. "They used to say I was a pretty little fellow. I lay in a velvet-covered basket in the living room. Mistress used to stroke me and play with me. But then I grew bigger and now I have to sleep in the kitchen. I do have a big pillow though and there's a stove – which at this time of year is the most beautiful thing in the world."

"Why is a stove beautiful?" asked the snowman. "Is it anything like me?"

The dog gave a little gruff laugh. "It's quite the opposite of you," he explained. "It is jet black, with a long pipe for a neck. It eats firewood, then fire spouts out of its mouth. I sit by its side – or sometimes under it – and it's so lovely and warm and comfortable. Look, you can see it through that window over there!"

The snowman shuffled over to the window and peered through. He saw a smooth, polished object with a long pipe. It was just about the same size as he was. He listened carefully and he could hear it crackling, just as he crackled in the cold. The flicker from the stove's fire reached out to him, and he felt wonderfully happy. The snowman gazed joyfully into the room where the stove stood on its three legs.

"Something has started to burn inside me!" he said. "How I long to get inside there, next to that stove. Surely it's not very much to ask for! If only I could get in there!"

"Don't be silly – you will never get in there," said the dog, "and if you were to reach the stove, you would disappear."

For the whole day the snowman stood looking through the window.

The Snowman

When evening began to fall, the room seemed even more inviting to him. The stove gave out a very gentle light, not at all like the cold beam of the moon or the hot blaze of the sun. And when the door of the room was opened, the stove flared up – it flickered rosily on the snowman's white face. "Oh, how beautiful the stove looks!" he cried. "I can't stand it any longer. How I wish I could get in there and be close to it!"

It was a long night, but the snowman didn't notice. He just stood there, lost in his thoughts of the wonderful stove. He didn't even notice himself crackling with the cold.

In the morning, the room's window panes were completely frosted over. They were covered with the most beautiful swirls and patterns of ice. But to the snowman they weren't beautiful at all, for they stopped him from seeing into the room and gazing at the stove.

The sun rose high in the sky and shone hotter than it had done the day before, but the snowman didn't say anything – he didn't complain once. All he could think of was the beautiful stove – it was so near to him and yet so far away. What a wonderful feeling it gave him!

Little by little he began to drip and melt away… until there was nothing left except a broom stuck upright in the ground – for the boys had built the snowman around it.

"Ah, now I see why he loved the stove so much," barked the dog. "That's the broom they use to sweep the stove out with…"

And when the broom was taken back inside, no one even noticed the snowman was gone.

The Elf Hill

Long ago, there was a very old tree which grew on an even older hill. Nobody knew that the hill was the home of the elves – and the elf king himself. Only the wild creatures nearby knew the secret…

One day, a few large lizards were lazing around under the tree, chatting to each other. "What a rumbling there is in the elf hill," said one of the lizards. "There's been such a noise for the past two days and nights that I haven't been able to get any sleep!"

"There's definitely something going on in there," said another lizard.

"I've just spoken to an earthworm," said a third lizard. "Even though he is blind and can't see, he has heard a great deal. The elves are having a ball, with very important guests. The elf king has ordered all the young elves to be there, to dance. And they are polishing all their gold treasure – they are going to put it out on display in the moonlight."

The Elf Hill

At that very moment, there was a loud *CRACK!* The elf hill split and opened, allowing the lizards to peep inside. Out came an old elf lady – the king's housekeeper. She hurried over to a beady-eyed raven waiting on a tree stump nearby.

"Could you deliver these invitations for me?" she asked the bird, handing him a bundle of envelopes.

"Croak," said the raven, and off he flew.

By the time evening fell, the great hall in the elf king's palace had been splendidly decorated – the floor had been washed with moonshine and the walls rubbed with magic ointment so they glowed in the dark. In the royal kitchen, all sorts of delicious foods were nearly prepared. And the old elf king had put on his best cloak, which shone like starlight.

"Father," said his youngest daughter, "you haven't told anybody who is coming tonight – will you tell me now, *please*?"

"Well, I suppose I should," he said. "You and your sisters are old enough to get married now. And the goblin king from Norway, who owns many stone castles and a huge gold mine, has two sons who are each looking for a

wife. I thought if we held a ball, we could introduce you to them."

At that moment two will-o'-the-wisps came jumping in. "They are coming!" they cried excitedly.

"Give me my crown," said the elf king, "and go and fetch your sisters."

The goblin king wore a thick bearskin and great warm boots. He stood outside the elf hill with his two sons.

"Call that a hill?" sneered the youngest.

"Yes," agreed the older brother, "back in Norway we'd just call it a hole!"

"Boys," said the king, "be careful or people will think you have got no manners."

They entered the elf hill and were

welcomed to the elf king's palace, where the great hall was packed with guests. The sea king was there with his mermaids and mermen, and there were imps and dwarves and hobgoblins. Everyone behaved themselves beautifully – except the two goblin princes from Norway. They sat straight down and put their feet up on the table!

"Feet off!" cried the goblin king.

The boys obeyed, but sulkily. They amused themselves by tickling the serving-girl elves with the fir cones they had in their pockets, and then took off their stinky boots and gave them to the poor girls to look after.

Their father was very different. The goblin

king told fine tales about the rocks of Norway
and the many waterfalls which crashed over
them. He told of how the salmon leap in the
rushing waters, while the water-god plays on
his golden harp. He spoke of the bright
winter nights, when boys skate with burning
torches across the smooth ice and sleighs
glide along with their bells jingling. He
described everything so clearly, that those
who listened could see it all.

While the guests ate, the young elves
danced – first in the usual way, and then
with loud stamping feet, and they performed
very well.

Then the elf king called his eldest daughter
to him. The goblin king and his sons watched

as she put a white pebble in her mouth and vanished instantly!

"Eeurgh!" said the eldest goblin prince. "I wouldn't want a wife of mine to keep disappearing all the time."

Then the elf king called forward his second daughter. She could conjure up a figure just like herself, which followed her around like a shadow.

"Eeew!" said the younger goblin prince. "One wife would be enough to deal with – who would want two!"

The third daughter was very different. She had learned how to decorate elfin puddings with tasty glow-worms.

"Now, she would make a good wife," said the goblin king, but his two sons just rolled their eyes.

Then came the fourth daughter. She brought a large harp with her, and when she struck the first chord everyone found they had to do whatever she wanted.

"This lady is beautiful but

dangerous," chuckled the goblin king – but he was speaking to thin air, because his two sons had had enough and stomped off out of the elf hill.

"Never mind – what can your last daughter do?" asked the goblin king, for he was enjoying himself thoroughly.

"I can tell stories," the elf princess explained, "as many as you like, about whatever you like."

"Here are my five fingers," said the goblin king. "Tell me a story for each of them."

So she held his hand and told him a wonderful story for each of the first three fingers, and he laughed till he nearly choked. When the elf princess came to the fourth finger, there was a gold ring on it. The goblin king said, "Take this ring and keep it – I will have you as a wife for myself!" Everyone clapped and cheered, and the goblin king looked around. "But where are my lads?" he asked.

Where indeed were they? The goblin king found them outside the elf hill, running around the fields and blowing out the will-o'-the-wisps' torches.

"What mischief have you been up to?" said the goblin king, dragging them back into the elf hill and the great hall. "I have chosen a bride – now it's your turn." The two goblin princes muttered and pulled faces.

But at that very moment the old elf

housekeeper announced: "The cockerel is crowing and dawn is here! We must close the shutters, or the rising sun will scorch us."

And with a *CRASH!* the elf hill closed up.

That was the last that anyone ever glimpsed of the goings on inside the elf hill.

"I really liked that goblin king," said the earthworm.

"I thought his sons were great!" said his lizard friend.

The earthworm sighed, shaking his head.

The Snail and the Rose Tree

Once upon a time, in a land far away, there was a beautiful garden. It was surrounded by a hedge of hazel-bushes, heavy with hazelnuts. Beyond the hedge were fields and meadows in which cows and sheep grazed peacefully. And in the middle of the garden a rose tree stood in full bloom. Under the blooming rose tree sat a tiny snail, thinking to himself.

"Just wait," he muttered under his breath. "One day I will show everyone! I will do much better things than grow roses like this tree, or bear nuts like that hedge, or give milk and wool like those cows and sheep."

"How exciting!" replied the rose tree. "I can't wait to see what you will do. Can I ask when you are going to do it?"

"Well, as you may have noticed, I take my time," remarked the snail. "The problem with you lot is you are always in such a hurry. You always get on with things straight away, and

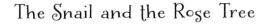

then no one has anything left to look forward to or get excited about!" With that, he pulled himself inside his shell and refused to say a word more. Days passed by, which turned to

weeks, which turned to months… and summer faded to autumn. The little snail crept deep underground and wasn't seen again until springtime. The following summer, the snail crept once again into the dappled sunshine under the rose tree. He raised his head half out of his shell, stretched out his horns, and then drew them in again.

"Everything looks just like it did last year," he moaned. "Nothing has changed, or happened that was any better than before. The rose tree is still bearing roses, the same as last year."

Again, the summer passed and the autumn came. The rose tree bore beautiful roses and buds until the weather became raw and cold, and the snow fell. The rose tree bowed its head and the snail crept into the ground.

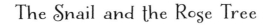

When spring began, the roses came out again – and the snail slowly came out too.

"You are an old rose tree now," the snail announced, shortly. "Why don't you hurry up and die? You have given the world everything you had to give – and I'm not sure that it was actually much use! How useful are roses, I wonder? I think if I had been you, I would have grown something much more useful… Anyway, you will soon be nothing but a large stick. Do you have anything to say for yourself?"

"Stop it! You are frightening me," said the rose tree. "I've never thought of things that way at all."

"No, I don't suppose you have," scolded

the cross little snail. "You have probably never taken the trouble to think at all. I mean, have you ever thought about why you bloom, and how it happens, and why it is that you bear roses and nothing else?"

"No," said the rose tree in a small voice. "I bloomed because I felt so glad about everything. The sun shone and warmed me and the air was so refreshing. I drank the pure dew and the cool rain and I lived, I breathed. I felt power rising out of the earth and surging up inside me, and strength and energy from up above tingling in my leaves and flowing down into my branches. I felt happier and happier – and so I went on blooming… That has been my life – I couldn't have done anything any different."

"Well, I suppose that all sounds very pleasant," sniffed the snail.

"Yes, everything has been given to me," said the rose tree thoughtfully. "But it seems as though you have been even luckier. Nature has given even more to you. You always seem to be thinking so deeply, you must have been given the gift of a very clever mind. I am sure that one day you will astonish the world!"

"Astonish the world!" cried the snail. "I won't do any such thing! The world means absolutely nothing to me. What on earth have I got to do with the world? I am quite busy enough just thinking about myself and being me."

Then the rose tree was quiet for a
moment, thinking.

At last she said, "But shouldn't all of us

here on earth be the best that we can, in order to help others? I have only my roses to offer, it's true. But you – if you have been given such a clever mind, what are you going to use it for?"

"What am I going to use it for? *What am I going to use it for?*" spat the snail. "I am not intending to use it for anybody except myself. You can go on bearing roses – it's what you're good at. The hazel-bush can grow nuts, the cows can give milk and the sheep can give wool – they all have people to please and help. But I want nothing to do with anyone – the world is nothing to me."

And with that, he withdrew into his house and closed up the entrance after him.

"How sad!" said the rose tree. "I could not creep into myself even if I wanted to. I have to go on growing roses. Then they drop their leaves and are blown away by the wind…"

But then, a memory struck the rose tree. "Yet once, I did see a woman put several of my roses into a bunch as a gift for a friend. And another time, a lady pinned one to her wedding dress. And I also remember a little girl picking one and kissing it and giving it to her mother. Those times made me so happy! They were the best in my life."

And the rose tree went on blooming, while the snail lay lazily in his house, wanting nothing to do with the world.

Years rolled by and eventually, the snail

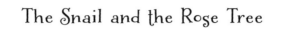

crumbled into the earth – and the rose tree too. In the garden, other rose trees bloomed, bringing happiness to many other people. And other snails crawled about, creeping into their houses and closing up the entrances tight, seeing nothing at all.

LESSONS LEARNED

The Windmill

A long time ago, in a land far away, there stood on a hill a stately windmill. It had been there as long as anyone could remember and looked rather like it was growing out of the countryside. People might

have thought that it just stood there with its sails creaking round and round and round, but in actual fact, the windmill spent its days thinking deeply.

"I am very lucky," she said to herself one morning, "that people like looking at me. To start with, I always have bright eyes. Either the sun's rays or the moonbeams shine at my windows, or the miller lights them up with candles and lanterns. I have four graceful wings – even the birds only have two. And I have a good set of millstones and wheels in my chest. There is a gallery that runs like a patterned belt around my stomach, and in my heart, the miller and his wife live. Their little children are like thoughts that run around my head. Indeed, the family keep me alive – I remember that lately I had to let the miller and his boys examine my millstones and wheels, to see what was going on there, for something was wrong. They knew just how to make me better, of course. Then the youngest climbed up into my hat and shouted out, and it tickled me!

"Out in the world, I can't see anything else like me. I can see houses but they just look wingless and strange.

"I have been here for many years and seen many things. And I know that the days pass, and the days come, and the time will arrive when I will become old and tumble down. But I will be built up again, newer and better.

216

I will look different, but as long as I have the miller and his wife living at my heart, and the children running

around me like thoughts, I will be the same deep down inside. And everyone will say: 'There's the mill on the hill – what a sight to see.'"

And so the days passed, and the days came, and one afternoon the windmill caught fire. The flames shot up and whipped in and out. They licked beams and planks and ate them up. The mill crumbled to ash and thick smoke rose from the embers until the wind carried it all away.

Very luckily, the miller's family had not been at home at the time. They were filled with sadness to lose the old mill, but they soon built a beautiful new mill, even better than the first. And the miller and his wife lived at the heart of the new mill and their little children ran around it like thoughts. Its windows were always brightly lit, and its sails creaked steadily round and round while it

stood there, thinking deeply. And everyone said: "There's the mill on the hill – what a sight to see."

The Emperor's New Clothes

Many years ago there lived an emperor who loved new clothes. He spent all his money on them. He didn't care about palaces, armies, or travelling abroad – all he was interested in was looking good.

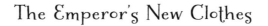

He had a different outfit for every hour of the day and was always to be found in his enormous dressing room, admiring himself in front of gigantic mirrors.

The emperor's home city was huge and bustling – every day people came from all over the world to do business and see the sights. One day, two men arrived from a far-off land who said they were weavers, but not ordinary weavers – the most amazing weavers in the world. They could weave cloth with astounding colours and patterns – but only clever people could see it. To anyone who was stupid, or not good enough for their job, it was invisible!

When news of the incredible fabric

reached the emperor's ears, he decided he must have some at once! 'If I wore clothes made of that magic material, I would be able to tell who among my subjects was clever and who was stupid,' he thought to himself, his eyes gleaming.

The emperor summoned the two weavers and gave them a huge sum of money so they could buy what they needed and get going. They straight away demanded the finest silk and the most expensive gold and silver thread. Then the emperor provided them with a room in the palace to work in, which was set up with two looms. He gave all his servants strict instructions that the weavers were to have whatever they asked for and

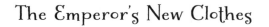

were not to be disturbed.

Then the two men began their work. Everyone was extremely curious and excited. News of what was going on had spread throughout the entire city, and all the people couldn't wait to see the beautiful fabric and find out just how clever or stupid their neighbours were. Inside the palace, the servants gave themselves all sorts of tasks and errands which would take them down the corridor past the room where the weavers were hard at work.

"They are very busy," they whispered to each other. "We can hear their shuttles flying along non-stop!" But if anyone was lucky enough to get a glimpse inside the workroom,

they were shocked. Instead of seeing stunning colours and amazing patterns, they saw nothing at all. The looms appeared to be empty! Of course, no one said anything to anyone else, because they did not want to be thought stupid. Instead, they would say: "I got a peep at the weavers' fabric and it was truly enchanting!" or "Those weavers are brilliant you know, their fabric is beyond compare!" And so all sorts of rumours spread about the miraculous cloth and interest built to a fever pitch, until the people of the city could talk of nothing else.

After weeks of waiting, the weavers sent out news that the fabric was ready. The emperor was desperate to see it, but he forced himself to wait – after all, seeing it on the loom would be a wonderful surprise, but seeing it for the first time when it was made up into clothes would be even better.

So the weavers called for scissors and pins and shut themselves away to make the finest outfit the emperor had ever owned. Each night they filled their workroom with candles so they could stay up late, cutting and sewing.

At last, the weavers announced they were finished. As they were ushered into the emperor's dressing room, he could hardly contain his excitement. Balanced on the weavers' outstretched hands were large, flat parcels of tissue paper that appeared to be as delicate as gossamer and as light as air. The weavers laid them out extremely carefully.

"Are you ready, your imperial majesty?" they asked the emperor, who was far too thrilled to speak. He just nodded and clapped his hands. The two weavers delicately opened the tissue paper parcels and stood back so the emperor could admire his new clothes.

"Well, what do you think?" they asked. "Aren't they splendid? Look at the detail of the patterning on the jacket and the rich colours in the trousers. Notice how the threads of the shirt shimmer and shine in different lights. See the contrasting stitching along the collar and pockets, and regard how the cloak flows. These really are the most handsome clothes in all your empire!"

The emperor stood there, stunned. He could see nothing at all! 'This is terrible!' he thought to himself. 'Am I stupid? Am I not fit to be emperor?' His heart thumped away in his chest in a panic and little beads of sweat broke out on his forehead.

"Erm… um…" he said, and he cleared his

throat, trying to find his voice. "Ahem… Yes! Yes! I see it all. The fabric is indeed most wonderful. The clothes are truly marvellous – miraculous even. Oh yes, gorgeous – really gorgeous. Thank you, thank you." And the emperor went on giving compliments as the weavers held up the jacket and shirt and trousers for him to admire, while he saw nothing but thin air between their hands.

The weavers were highly pleased. The emperor awarded each of them a medal to wear on their chest and announced that from then on, they each had the title of Imperial Court Weaver. He paid them a fortune for their work and the two men went away bowing, most delighted.

Then it was time for the emperor to put his new outfit on. There was to be a special procession through the city, so everyone could see and admire the weavers' work. The emperor took off his clothes and his closest and wisest advisors pretended to help him dress in each of the new garments – for they couldn't see anything either!

The emperor turned round and round in front of his mirrors. "Well, I suppose I am ready…" he said, nervously. "How do I look?"

"Stunning, your excellency," his advisors assured him, and they pretended to pick up the end of his cloak and followed him out into the streets.

How everyone gasped and clapped as the

emperor paraded along! "Wonderful, your grace! What style!" the crowd called out, although they couldn't see anything at all.

Then all of a sudden a little child's voice piped up, calling out: "But he has nothing on!"

Whispers rustled through the crowd like fire: "He has nothing on! The emperor has nothing on!"

The emperor shivered, for it seemed that they were right, although he could not admit it. He lifted his head higher and walked even more proudly, and the wise advisors held on tighter to the cloak that wasn't there at all.

The Farmyard Cockerel and the Weathercock

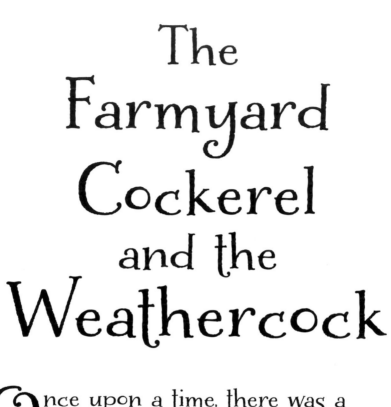

Once upon a time, there was a cucumber growing in the vegetable patch of a farmhouse. She was wondering who was the most useful – the handsome farmyard cockerel or the weathercock that sat on top of the farmhouse roof.

The cucumber pondered over the question for a long time. Then she decided: "I suppose it has to be the farmyard cockerel who is more useful. After all, he wakes everyone up in the morning with his proud *cockadoodledoo*. But the weathercock can't even creak, let alone crow. The weathercock doesn't have hens, nor chicks, he just sits up there and thinks of himself.

"Yes, the more I think of it, the answer has to be that the farmyard cockerel is best. Every step he takes looks like a dance! Every *cockadoodledoo* sounds like music!" And so the cucumber rested in the vegetable patch, content with her decision.

That very night, there was a terrible storm. The wind howled loudly and rain lashed down. The hens, the chicks, and even the farmyard cockerel trembled as they sheltered in their wooden houses.

However, even though the weathercock was at the top of the farmhouse roof, in the thick of the storm, he sat firm. He did not even turn round, because he was old and had become stiff and rusty through spinning to tell the wind direction for so many years. He just sat with his head held high in the black storm clouds, and was lit up every now and again by bright flashes of lightning.

Next morning, when the sky was clear and the sun was out, the little birds all came out of their hiding places to go swooping and diving through the air.

"How silly they all are," muttered the weathercock as he watched them fluttering here and there. "The pigeons are fat and only think about filling themselves with food. The swallows are good at telling stories of all their adventures in warm foreign lands, but they say the same ones over and over again – they get boring after a while. And those thrushes can't stop whistling – it gets on my nerves!"

The weathercock did not want to be friends with any of the little birds. "The world is no good," he grumbled. "Everything in it is just stupid."

Then the cockerel and the hens and chicks

came strutting into the farmyard.
"Cockadoodledoo!" the cockerel crowed.
"My chicks will grow up big and strong, just
like their father." And the hens and chicks
clucked and chirped. "What a champion of
cockerels I am!" he crowed, and with that, he
flapped his wings and made his comb swell
up, and he crowed again.

"That farmyard cockerel is stupid
too," the weathercock said to himself.
"What is he good for? He can't even lay
an egg!"

But then there came a mighty gust of
wind and the weathercock snapped right off.
His rusty old fixings had been put to great
strain in the storm. Now they could no

longer do their job and hold him up. He
tumbled to the ground and lay there while
the cockerel, the hens and the chicks pecked

237

and scratched around him.

And the moral of the story is: You're no use to anyone if you wear yourself out!

The
Fir Tree

Out in the forest stood a pretty little fir tree. He grew in a lovely sunny spot, but he was not happy. He longed to grow tall, like all the other firs round about. Sometimes little children would come by, gathering strawberries and raspberries. They would say, "Oh how sweet that little tree is!" – but it just made the tree really fed up.

"Oh, if only I were as tall as the other trees," sighed the little fir, "I would spread my branches far around and look out over the whole wide world. The birds would nest in me and when the wind blew I could nod grandly like the others."

Months passed and the little fir took no pleasure in the sunshine, the birds and the clouds that went sailing over him morning and evening. Then winter came, and the snow lay all around, white and sparkling. A hare often came bounding along and would spring right over him. It made him so angry!

But by the time two more winters had passed, the little fir had grown. The hare could no longer leap over him.

'To grow up and become old and important – that's the best thing in the world,' thought the tree.

Every autumn, woodcutters came and felled a few of the largest trees. Each year, as the little fir grew taller, he shuddered with fear when it happened. For the great, stately trees fell to the ground with a crash and their branches were cut off. Then they were laid on carts and horses dragged them away out of the wood. 'Where are they going?' the fir tree always wondered.

"Enjoy being young!" the sunbeams told him, and the wind gave him kisses – but the tree just shrugged them off.

When Christmas time came around, still more trees were felled – sometimes quite young ones, even smaller than the fir tree, now he had grown. The woodcutters never hacked off their branches – but still, they were loaded onto carts and horses dragged them away. "What happens to them?" the fir tree thought aloud.

"We know!" chirped the swallows. "People take them into their houses and decorate

them with colourful ornaments and brightly shining candles. They are so beautiful!"

"If only I could be one of them one day," sighed the fir.

"Be content here in the fresh woodland," said the raindrops.

"It is better out here with us," squeaked the squirrels.

But the fir could not be content. He longed to be elsewhere – and he grew and grew and grew.

The next Christmas time, the fir tree was felled before any of the others. He was taken away into a yard where there were hundreds of other felled trees. Then a man came and picked him out and carried him off to his house. Inside, he was placed in a big tub, in a warm room, and all around him were chairs, vases and pictures.

How the tree trembled with excitement! What was to happen now?

Children soon came and decorated him, until he sparkled and glittered and gleamed. He stood tall and proud at first, but after a few days, his branches grew so tired with holding up all the decorations that he developed quite a backache! 'When will this be over?' he wondered.

Then one afternoon people flocked into the

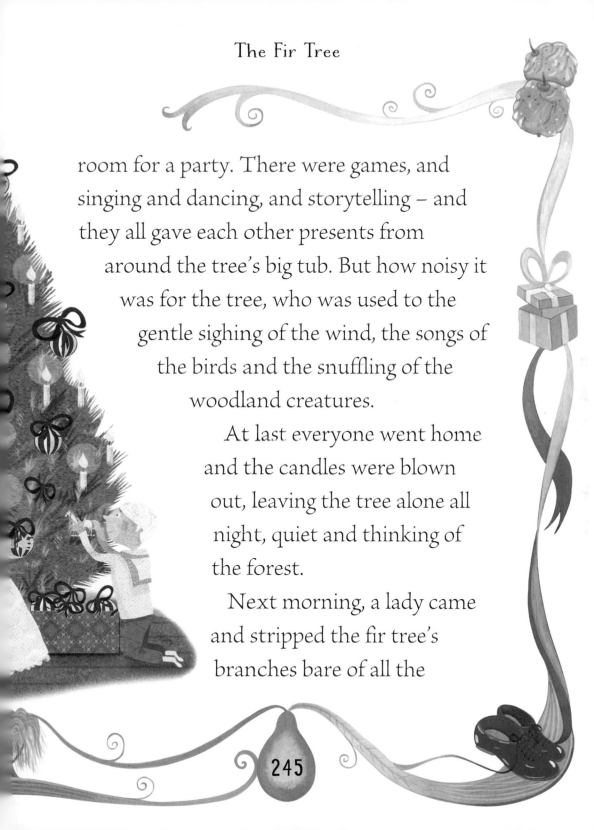

room for a party. There were games, and
singing and dancing, and storytelling – and
they all gave each other presents from
around the tree's big tub. But how noisy it
was for the tree, who was used to the
gentle sighing of the wind, the songs of
the birds and the snuffling of the
woodland creatures.

At last everyone went home
and the candles were blown
out, leaving the tree alone all
night, quiet and thinking of
the forest.

Next morning, a lady came
and stripped the fir tree's
branches bare of all the

decorations. She wrapped them up in newspaper and packed them away into boxes. Then the man who had brought the tree to the house heaved him up out of the tub. He dragged him outside into the courtyard and flung him into a corner among some nettles and weeds.

"At last, I am outside again!" said the tree to himself. He stretched out his branches towards the pale winter sunshine, but alas! They had become brown and dry. His needles dropped off and fell like rain to the ground. "Oh, I wish had made the most of life when I was younger," he sighed. "Everyone told me to be happy, but I just wanted to grow up. Now I am old – and I haven't

stopped to enjoy anything at all."

Next day, a boy came and chopped the tree into little pieces for the fire.

The tree's life was past – and the story is past too, for that's the way with all stories.

The Money Pig

In the nursery, lots of toys were lying about. There were teddy bears and building blocks, drawing pencils and toy soldiers, a dolls' house and a train set. High up on top of a cupboard was a china money box, in the shape of a pig. It had a slit in its back so coins could be dropped into it, and a stopper in its tummy so they wouldn't fall out again. It was so stuffed full of coins that when you shook it, it no longer rattled.

The money pig was very proud of itself, for being full is the highest rank that a money box can achieve. It knew very well that what it had in its stomach would have bought all the other toys – and they knew it too.

One night, when the family who lived in the house were sound asleep, one of the dolls suggested excitedly, "Shall we play a game of Men and Women?"

Everyone thought this was a splendid idea. All the toys jumped up and down in

excitement shouting, "Yes! Yes! Let's!"
Even the children's go-cart
wanted to join in the fun.

The only toy who didn't
reply was the money pig.
He was far too grand to let
himself go and call out like
that. So the others wrote
him a special note,
inviting him to join
the game.

"I haven't
decided yet if I
will or won't
join in," the
money pig

250

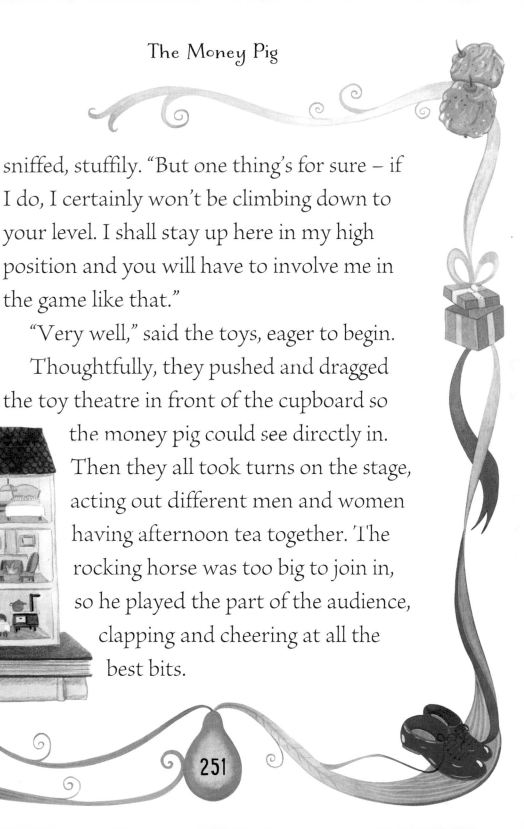

sniffed, stuffily. "But one thing's for sure – if
I do, I certainly won't be climbing down to
your level. I shall stay up here in my high
position and you will have to involve me in
the game like that."

"Very well," said the toys, eager to begin.
Thoughtfully, they pushed and dragged
the toy theatre in front of the cupboard so
the money pig could see directly in.
Then they all took turns on the stage,
acting out different men and women
having afternoon tea together. The
rocking horse was too big to join in,
so he played the part of the audience,
clapping and cheering at all the
best bits.

That was what they called 'playing Men and Women'. All the toys enjoyed themselves immensely – although now and again they did wonder what the money pig thought of it all, for he stayed aloof and silent on the cupboard.

In fact, the money pig wasn't thinking of them at all. He was too busy dreaming about all the expensive, precious things he could buy with all the money in his tummy.

In fact, it would have been much better if he had climbed down from his high position and joined in with the game because all of a sudden – BAM! – someone bumped into the cupboard. The money pig toppled off and was smashed to pieces on the ground. The

silver and gold coins hopped and danced and rolled along the floor, but the money pig stayed quite still and lifeless.

Next day, the family swept up all the broken bits of the proud money pig and put them in the bin. By afternoon, a brand new money pig was standing on top of the cupboard – its tummy completely empty and

waiting to be filled up with coins.

That was a new beginning – and so with that we will make an end.

What the Old Man Does is Always Right

Once upon a time, there lived an old couple in a cosy farmhouse with a thatched roof. They did not own much, but one thing they did have was a horse, which lived on the grass near the roadside. The old farmer often rode into town upon this horse. His neighbours sometimes borrowed it too.

But the time came when the farmer thought that the horse was becoming too old and tired and slow. "Maybe we should sell the horse," he said to his wife, "or swap him for something else."

"You know best, old man," said the wife. "It's market day today, so ride into town and do whatever you think – you're always right."

She kissed him, and away he rode upon the horse that was going to be sold or swapped for something else.

The road was very dusty, for many people were going along it to get to the market. Among the crowds of travellers a man came trudging along, leading a cow. The farmer thought the cow was as beautiful as any cow could be. "I bet she gives good milk," he said to himself. "I know cows aren't worth as much as horses, but I think it would still be a good exchange." And he called out to the man, "Hello there – you with the cow! Would you like to swap it for my horse?"

The man answered, "To be sure, I will," and so the exchange was made.

The farmer could have turned straight back then. But, having made up his mind to go to the market, he thought he would do so anyway. Off he went with his cow alongside him. After a short time, he overtook a man who was leading a sheep. It was a good, fat sheep with a fine fleece on its back.

"That fleece would keep us warm in the winter," the farmer said to himself. He called out to the man, "Good morning! Would you like to swap your sheep for my cow?"

"Certainly," replied the man, and the exchange was made.

The farmer carried on down the road to market. But before too long he overtook another man, who was carrying a large goose under his arm.

"What a heavy creature you have there," said the farmer. "It has plenty of feathers and plenty of fat. Shall we exchange? My sheep for your goose?"

"Very well," said the man, and the exchange was made.

By this time the farmer had arrived at the town gate. The gatekeeper was standing there with a hen tied to the gate by a string, so it would not run off into the crowd and get lost. As soon as the farmer saw it he thought, 'Why that's the finest hen I've ever seen. I bet it lays wonderful eggs.' And he asked the gatekeeper if he would swap the hen for his goose.

"Willingly," said the gatekeeper, and once

again the exchange was made.

Now the farmer had done a great deal of business on his way to the market, and he was hot and tired. He wanted to sit and rest, and have something to eat and drink, so he made his way towards an inn. He was just about to enter when a man came out carrying a heavy sack. "What have you got there?" asked the farmer.

"Rotten apples," answered the man, "a whole sackful of them. They will do to feed the pigs."

"Why that would be a terrible waste," the farmer replied. "I would like to take them home to my wife. Last year our old apple tree bore only one apple, and my wife kept it in

the cupboard till it was quite withered and rotten. How happy she would be if I took her a whole sackful! Will you swap your sack of rotten apples for my hen?"

The man's eyes twinkled with delight. "Of course I will," he said, and so the exchange was made.

Finally, the farmer entered the inn with the sack of apples.

"What's in the sack?" asked the innkeeper, and the farmer told him the whole story of the horse, which he had exchanged for a cow, which he had exchanged for a sheep, and all the rest of it, right down to the apples.

"Well, you'll be in big trouble with your wife when you get home," said the innkeeper, shaking his head. "Fancy leaving with a horse and returning with nothing but a sack of rotten apples!"

"I won't be in trouble," said the farmer, "she'll kiss me and say, 'What the old man does is always right'."

"Let's bet on it then," said the innkeeper. "I'll bet you a bag of gold coins that you'll be in big trouble."

"Deal," said the farmer, although he didn't even have a single gold coin, let alone a whole bag of them.

The innkeeper summoned his coach and the two men drove to the farmer's house.

"Good evening, old woman," said the farmer cheerily.

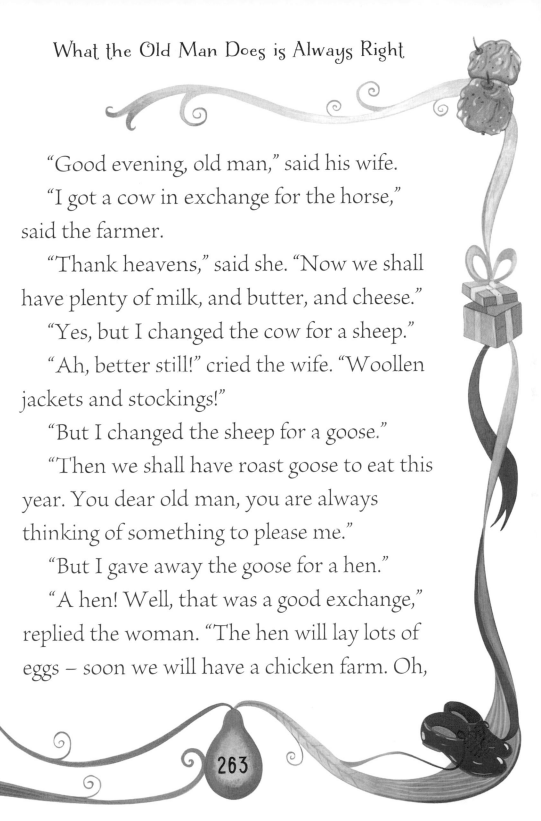

"Good evening, old man," said his wife.

"I got a cow in exchange for the horse," said the farmer.

"Thank heavens," said she. "Now we shall have plenty of milk, and butter, and cheese."

"Yes, but I changed the cow for a sheep."

"Ah, better still!" cried the wife. "Woollen jackets and stockings!"

"But I changed the sheep for a goose."

"Then we shall have roast goose to eat this year. You dear old man, you are always thinking of something to please me."

"But I gave away the goose for a hen."

"A hen! Well, that was a good exchange," replied the woman. "The hen will lay lots of eggs – soon we will have a chicken farm. Oh, this is just what I was wishing for."

"Yes, but I exchanged the hen for a sack of rotten apples."

"What! I really must give you a kiss for that!" exclaimed the wife. "My dear, good husband, as soon as you left this morning, I began to think of what I could cook you for supper. I decided on fried eggs and bacon, with some sweet herbs. Now, I had eggs and bacon, but no herbs. So I went across the road to the schoolmaster's house, for I knew his wife had plenty of herbs. I begged her to lend me a handful, but she was very mean indeed.

"'Lend!' she exclaimed. 'I have nothing to lend; nothing at all grows in our poor garden.

I could not even lend you a shrivelled apple, my dear woman.'

"But now, I can lend her a whole sackful, which I'm very happy about – it makes me laugh just to think about it! Well done, old man – whatever you do is always right!" And then she gave him a hearty kiss.

"Well, I never," said the innkeeper, greatly surprised. Shaking his head in disbelief, he handed over

to the couple a bag full of gold coins.

And so the farmer and his wife lived happily ever after.

The Buckwheat

From its name, buckwheat sounds as if it should be a cereal, like wheat or rye. But it is not a grain. It is not even a grass. It is in fact a flowering wild plant with seeds that can be used in cooking or ground down to make flour.

I f you come across a field of buckwheat after there has been a violent thunderstorm, very often it looks blackened and burned, as if it has been briefly set on fire. People who live in the countryside say that it gets singed in the lightning. But sparrows say that the lightning strikes it down on purpose.

The sparrows told me once that they heard the real reason why from a willow tree. He is a very old and distinguished willow tree, and completely to be trusted – even if he does look rather crippled by age. His trunk has split and brambles and grass have taken root there. The tree stoops forward slightly and the branches hang quite down to the ground,

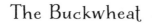

just like wispy strands of green hair.

Today in the surrounding fields different types of corn grow there – not only rye and barley but also oats. The oats are the prettiest; when the grains are ripe they look like little golden canary-birds sitting on a bough. But all the corn looks beautiful, standing and smiling in the sunshine. When the ears are heavy with grain they bend and nod humbly.

Once, long ago, a field of buckwheat grew there too, exactly opposite the old willow tree. But the buckwheat did not bend like the grain. Instead, it stood up straight and stiff, holding its head up proudly.

"I am just as important as all the corn,"

one of the buckwheat plants remarked boastfully to the willow tree one day, "and I must say, I am *much* more beautiful! My flowers are as pretty as apple blossom. It's quite a delight to look at me and my family. You must agree, old willow tree. Do you know of any plant prettier than we are?"

At that moment a breeze blew around the willow tree. He nodded his head and dipped his branches as if to say, 'Indeed I do.'

The buckwheat wasn't put off at all. In fact, the plant spread herself out even wider with pride. "Stupid tree!" she scoffed rudely. "He's so old and has been there so long that he's got grass sprouting out of his body!"

Time went by and one night, a terrible

storm blew up. The wind howled and plucked at the plants with strong fingers. The rain lashed down and battered them. All the plants in the cornfields hurried to fold up their leaves and bow their little heads, to try to avoid harm. But the buckwheat plants refused to do so. They simply stood up even straighter than ever.

"Bow down as we do," urged the other wildflowers, worriedly.

"Why should we?" replied the buckwheat.

"Bow down as we do," cried the ears of corn. "The angel of the storm is coming, and his wings spread from the sky above to the earth down below. He will cut you in half before you can even cry out."

"There's nothing that can make us bow down," stated the buckwheat brazenly. "We will not bow down to anyone or anything."

"Lovely buckwheat, please close your leaves and lower your flowers," begged the old willow tree. "And whatever you do, do not look at the lightning when it strikes. When the skies split open it gives us a little glimpse into heaven – but the sight is so dazzling that even

humans shouldn't gaze at it. It blinds them, so whatever would it do to us lesser beings?"

"Lesser beings, indeed!" snorted the buckwheat. "Of course we're good enough to look into heaven!" And boldly all the buckwheat looked straight up, while the lightning blazed across the sky as if the whole world were in flames.

When the terrifying storm had died away, the wildflowers and the corn gently raised their drooping heads. The air was still and pure to breathe, and they felt quite refreshed by the rain. However, the buckwheat was a sorry sight. The plants were scorched black by the lightning and lay like limp weeds across the earth.

The old willow tree waved its branches in the wind and large drops of water fell from his green leaves, just as if he were weeping.

"Why do you cry," asked the sparrows, "when everything else is cheerful? Look, the sun is smiling and the clouds are floating in the blue. Can't you smell the beautiful scent of growing things? Tell us why you are weeping, old willow tree."

Then the willow told the sparrows why the buckwheat had met its sad end – that the lightning had punished it for its pride.

The Buckwheat

And this is the tale that the sparrows told me, in turn, one evening when I begged them to give me a story…

Good Luck Can Lie in a Button

Now I will tell you a story about good luck. We all know what it is like to be lucky. Some people know good luck day in, day out. Other people sometimes have a run of good luck that lasts for a little while, now

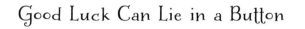

and then. And other people are only lucky just once in their whole life. But at some time or other, good luck comes to us all.

Everyone knows that it's God who sends babies to their parents. He might send a baby to a family in a house in a city, or a farmhouse in the countryside, or a royal castle, or a poor cottage. But what you may not know is that when God sends the baby, he always leaves it with a gift of good luck. He doesn't put the luck where the child is born, he hides it away somewhere in the world where you would least expect to find it. But sooner or later, it is always found.

For instance, it may be hidden in an apple – as it was for a man called Newton. An apple once fell into his lap, and his luck came with it. If you don't know the story, then ask someone who does to tell it to you. I've got another story for you – a story about a pear.

There was once a man who was born into a very poor family. He grew up very poor and by the time he got married, he still hadn't got a penny. He was an umbrella-maker, but he scarcely made enough money for food.

"Oh, I'll never find my luck," he often said.

The man lived in a tiny cottage with a little garden around it. Thickets of sour wild berries grew there, as well as a pear tree. It had never borne any fruit, yet the man's luck lay hidden inside it.

One night, there was a terrible storm with

278

a howling gale. It said in the newspapers the following day that the wind was so strong it lifted a big stagecoach off the road and threw it aside as if it were a shoebox. So the man wasn't surprised to find that a big branch had been torn from his pear tree. He heaved the branch into his workshop and, just for fun, he carved wooden pears out of it – big, medium and small ones. "Look, our tree has given us pears for once," he said to his children, laughing, and he handed the wooden pears to them to play with.

Now, everyone who lives in a country where it rains a lot needs an umbrella. But even though the man was an umbrella-maker, his family had only one umbrella between them – they had had to sell all the rest to get money for food. Their umbrella was old and worn out. When the wind blew hard, it would turn inside out. Sometimes one of the spokes would snap, so it was lucky that the man knew how to mend it.

However, the most annoying thing about the umbrella was to do with the button and loop that held it closed. Just as the umbrella was neatly folded and clasped shut, the

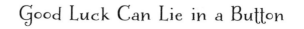

button would fly off without warning.

One day it popped off and the umbrella-maker searched for it everywhere. He was looking for it in the cracks in the floor when he came across one of the smallest pears he had given his children to play with. "Well," he said to himself, "if I can't find the button, maybe this will do." He poked a tiny hole in it and sewed it to the umbrella, and it fitted through the loop and buttoned it up to perfection. It was the best button that the umbrella-maker had ever made.

The man got on with making a new batch of umbrellas to be sent to a shop-owner in town. He made them all with small wooden pears as buttons.

The shop-owner soon sent back news that they had sold out in double-quick time! Customers loved the little wooden pears. They noticed that they held the umbrellas shut much better than buttons – and looked much more interesting too. The shop-owner put in an order for a new batch of umbrellas straight away – but this time, twice as many, and all with pear fasteners, of course.

The umbrella-maker was delighted. He used up the branch making little wooden pears – and the umbrellas kept selling and selling. He had to cut down the whole tree to make more. When that was used up, he bought some pear tree wood to make even more – for the umbrellas were flooding out of

the shop and money was flooding back to him. He was richer than he could ever have dreamed.

"My luck was in that pear tree all along," the man said. Soon he was able to open an umbrella-making factory with plenty of workers to help him. He was always happy and he replied to anyone who asked him why: "Good luck may lie in a button."

And I agree with him. In a country called Denmark, people say that if you put a white button in your mouth you'll turn invisible – although it must be the right sort of button, a lucky

button from God's own hand.

But I have already found my luck. I know it when I tell my stories and see children's eyes shine and grown-ups smile and laugh.

Now this is a true story. It really happened. I could tell you the man's town and country, but that isn't important. What is important is that you remember that your good luck can lie anywhere – even in a button. I hope you find it one day...

The
Red Shoes

Once upon a time, there lived a little girl called Karen who was very poor. Her family was so poor that they couldn't afford to buy proper shoes for her. In summer, little Karen ran around barefoot.

And in winter, she had to wear thick wooden shoes that rubbed her poor feet and ankles red raw.

In the middle of the village lived a shoemaker. The shoemaker's wife felt very sorry for little Karen. So she took some scraps of leftover red cloth and did her best to sew them into shoes for her.

Karen's mother was very ill, and just as the shoes were finished, the woman sadly died. The first time Karen got to wear her new shoes was at her mother's funeral, walking behind the coffin. The shoes weren't the right colour, of course, for they were too bright for a funeral, and they looked rather clumsy and odd – but Karen thought they were the best shoes in the world. Having them on her feet made her mother's funeral a little more bearable for her.

As the mourners trudged down the road on their way home, a fine carriage passed by. Inside was a rich old lady who caught sight of little Karen – thin and sad, in her rags and

poor shoes. The rich old lady felt so sorry for her that she asked if she could look after her.

And so Karen went to live with the old lady. The little girl was sure it was the red shoes which had brought her this piece of luck, but the old lady thought the shoes were dreadful and told her servants to burn them. Karen was given lovely new clothes and shoes, and people told her she was beautiful. When the little girl looked in the mirror, she saw such a pretty reflection that she could hardly believe it was her!

The rich old lady looked after Karen very well and taught her to read and write and sew. And when the queen and little princess visited their town, the rich old lady took

Karen to the castle to see if they could see
them. Karen stood among the cheering
crowds, wide-eyed as the princess came to
the window to let everyone admire her. The
princess was dressed in a lovely white silk
dress. She didn't wear a tiara or a train, but
she did wear a pair of shiny red patent leather
shoes. They were even prettier than the
ones that the shoemaker's wife had made
for Karen.

The next time the old lady took Karen to
the shoe shop, Karen insisted on choosing a
pair of shoes just like the ones the princess
had worn. The old lady couldn't see very well,
so although she realized they were very shiny,
she couldn't see that they were red. So when

Karen wanted to wear them to church that Sunday, the old lady didn't say no.

Of course, it wasn't right to wear showy colours like that to church! As Karen and the old lady walked up the aisle to find a seat, everyone stared in shock at Karen's feet. The little girl loved her shoes so much that she didn't care. She couldn't think of anything else. All the time she was meant to be saying her prayers and singing hymns, she was admiring her shiny red shoes.

When the service was over, several people came up to the old lady and told her that Karen's shoes were red. The old lady was extremely cross. She told Karen that it was very naughty to wear bright party shoes like

that to church and that, in the future, she
would have to wear her black ones, even
though they were old.

But when the next Sunday came around,
Karen looked at her old black shoes, and she
looked at her new shiny red shoes – and put
on the red ones. Once again, all Karen could
think of in church were her beautiful shoes.
She quite forgot to pray or sing. And all the
while, everyone's eyes were on her feet,
scolding her silently.

At the end of the service, the worshippers
came out of the church to find an old beggar-
man waiting in the porch. "Let me shine your
shoes for you," he was saying to everyone,
hoping to earn a few coins. The old lady

stretched out one foot, then the other, so the beggar-man could clean the dust off them. Then Karen did the same. "What pretty dancing shoes!" the beggar-man said to her. "Never come off when you dance," he told the shoes, and he tapped the sole of each of them with his hand.

Karen couldn't resist dancing a few steps, but once she began, her feet kept on dancing. She couldn't stop! It was as if the shoes were in control. She danced away from the church. The old lady's coachman had to run after her and catch her and lift her into the carriage. But even there, her feet went on dancing – her legs kicked out and hit the old lady, and she could do nothing about it!

When they reached home, Karen danced out of the carriage. She wanted to dance into the house, but her shoes danced the opposite way, down the street… and around the corner… and down the next street… and the next… and all the way out of the town. Dance she did, and dance she must, all the way into the dark woods.

Karen was terribly frightened and tried to kick off her shoes, but they seemed to be glued to her feet. So all she could do was dance, over fields and valleys, in the rain and the sun, by day and by night.

There was no rest for the little girl, who danced for weeks, until she finally danced right back into the church. There, she danced

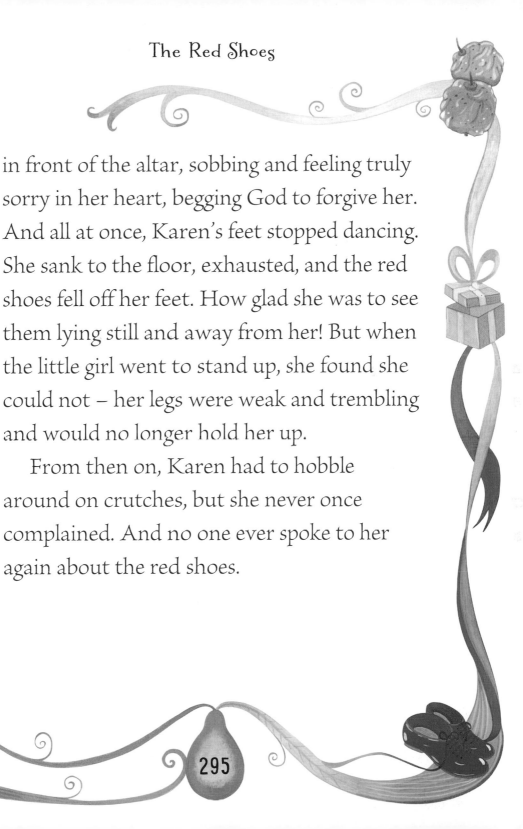

in front of the altar, sobbing and feeling truly sorry in her heart, begging God to forgive her. And all at once, Karen's feet stopped dancing. She sank to the floor, exhausted, and the red shoes fell off her feet. How glad she was to see them lying still and away from her! But when the little girl went to stand up, she found she could not – her legs were weak and trembling and would no longer hold her up.

From then on, Karen had to hobble around on crutches, but she never once complained. And no one ever spoke to her again about the red shoes.

The Swineherd

There was once a prince who was quite poor, as princes go. His kingdom was very small and he didn't have much treasure. Still, there were hundreds of princesses who would have been glad to

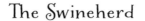

marry him – but he wanted to marry the daughter of the emperor himself.

The prince decided to send the emperor's daughter the very best presents he had to offer. In his garden there was a rose bush which only blossomed every five years – and then with just a single rose. But what a rose it was! Its perfume was so sweet that whoever smelled it forgot all their troubles.

A little bird often visited the rose bush. It sang so wonderfully that it was as if all the best music in the world was contained in its tiny throat.

The prince picked the special rose at full bloom and caught the wonderful bird, then he put them carefully in little silver cases and

sent them to the emperor's daughter.

The princess loved presents and she clapped her hands with joy. "I hope one is a necklace," she said.

Then out came the beautiful rose.

"How prettily it is made!" said all the ladies-in-waiting.

"It is more than pretty," said the emperor, "it is perfect."

But then the princess felt the rose's velvety petals and she began to cry. "It's real!" she howled. "What am I meant to do with a real rose? It will just fade and die."

"Tut tut!" scoffed all the ladies-in-waiting. "A sculpture or a painting of a rose would have been much better."

"Let's see what's in the other case before we get angry," soothed the emperor.

Then the little bird flew out and sang so beautifully that everyone nearly forgot to breathe while they were listening.

"It sounds just like my mother's musical box," said the princess, very pleased. Then her face fell. "But look, the bird is just dull and uninteresting – it's real too."

"Oh what a shame," sighed all the ladies-in-waiting. "It would have been much better if it was a toy in silver or gold."

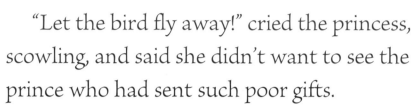

"Let the bird fly away!" cried the princess, scowling, and said she didn't want to see the prince who had sent such poor gifts.

When the prince heard the news, he wasn't at all put off. He disguised himself as a poor farm worker and went to ask for a job at the emperor's palace.

"Well, we need someone to look after the pigs…" the emperor said.

So the prince was appointed the emperor's swineherd. All day long, he tended the pigs in their stinky sties. But he spent the evenings at a very different type of work. Carefully, he hammered out a little metal pot with bells all around it. When the pot boiled, the bells played a sweet melody, and if you put your

finger in the steam you could smell what food was being cooked in each home in the city.

The princess was sitting at her window one day when she heard the sweet music floating to her on the breeze. She was enchanted and at once sent one of her ladies-in-waiting down to find out where it was coming from.

When the maid returned and told the princess the music was made by the swineherd's magic pot, the princess declared that she must have it at once. But then the lady-in-waiting looked down at her feet and blushed. "He said that the price for it is ten kisses," she whispered, shyly.

"How rude!" declared the princess. Then

she sighed. "Well, one of you maids will just have to go and kiss him then."

The ladies-in-waiting all gasped in shock, and the maid who had spoken to the swineherd grew even redder. "He said the kisses had to be from you, your highness," she squeaked.

"Oh fiddlesticks!" huffed the princess, very annoyed – but she really had to have that pot! "Well, you will all have to stand round me, so no one sees," she announced.

So the princess went down to the royal pigsties, where the swineherd was gleefully waiting. The ladies-in-waiting stood around the couple with their backs to them and held out their skirts, so they were hidden. Then

the princess gave the swineherd ten kisses
and he gave her the pot.

All day and into the night, the princess
and her ladies-in-waiting were fascinated by
the pot. They kept it boiling constantly –
they knew everything that was cooking in the
city and the music was delightful.

Then, a few days later, the princess heard
music floating up to her window once more.
She sent a lady-in-waiting outside to see
where it was coming from, and she came
back with the news that the swineherd had
made a magic rattle – whenever anyone
shook it, they could play any piece of music
ever composed.

"That's incredible!" the princess breathed,

her eyes wide. "How much does he want for it?"

"A hundred kisses!" the lady-in-waiting giggled.

"Oh botheration!" puffed the princess, very vexed – but she really had to have that magic rattle! So the princess went back down to the royal pigsties, where the swineherd was again gleefully waiting. The ladies-in-waiting all stood around the couple, and held out their skirts so they were hidden. Then the princess

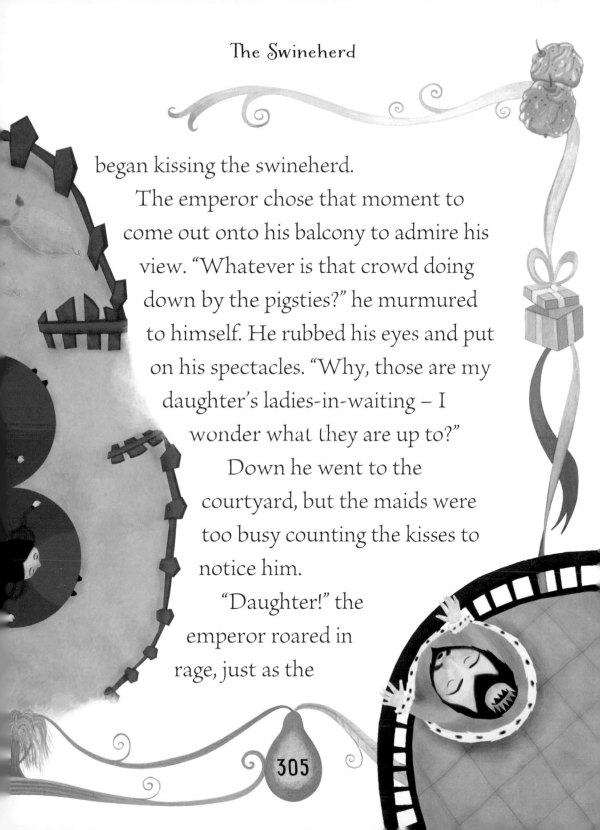

began kissing the swineherd.

The emperor chose that moment to come out onto his balcony to admire his view. "Whatever is that crowd doing down by the pigsties?" he murmured to himself. He rubbed his eyes and put on his spectacles. "Why, those are my daughter's ladies-in-waiting – I wonder what they are up to?"

Down he went to the courtyard, but the maids were too busy counting the kisses to notice him.

"Daughter!" the emperor roared in rage, just as the

swineherd was receiving the eighty-sixth kiss. "Stop that at once!"

He was so furious that he threw both the swineherd and his daughter straight out of his kingdom.

The couple stood outside the gates and the princess sobbed. "Oh why was I so foolish?" she wept. "I wish I had married the prince who sent me gifts after all!"

The swineherd went to a nearby stream and washed his face. He took off his shabby clothes, pulled his prince's garments out of his sack and put them on. Then he went back to comfort the princess.

He was now so handsome, she couldn't take her eyes off him!

"I am the prince who sent you the rose and the bird," he explained. "Now you have learnt your lesson, I forgive you for being so silly." And he took her back to his kingdom and married her, and they lived happily ever after.

308

FRIENDS AND ENEMIES

Thumbelina

There was once a woman who longed to have a tiny little child. An old witch gave her a barleycorn to plant, which grew into a large stem with a striking, brightly coloured bud, rather like a closed

tulip. The woman kissed its red-and-yellow petals and – *POP!* – the bud opened. In the middle sat a tiny girl, no taller than a thumb. So the woman called her Thumbelina.

Thumbelina was enchanting. She was dainty and beautiful, and when she sang, she had the sweetest voice ever heard. In the daytime, she liked to float on a dish of water in a tulip petal boat, and paddle back and forth. At night, she slept in a bed made of a polished walnut shell with a rose petal quilt.

One night, a horrid old mother toad came hopping in through an open window. The creature looked at the sleeping girl and thought, 'Here's the perfect wife for my son.' She picked up the walnut shell and hopped off with Thumbelina, out of the window and into the garden. A broad stream ran through it, and so the mother toad swam out into the middle of the water and laid the walnut shell, with Thumbelina still sleeping in it, upon a flat water lily leaf.

The next morning, when Thumbelina awoke and found she was a prisoner on a little island, she began to cry bitterly. Across the water, the mother toad and her son sat in the mud, scooping out a new home for him to live in with Thumbelina.

Thumbelina sank down on the water lily leaf, sobbing. She did not want to marry a toad and live in a nasty swamp.

The little fishes who lived in the stream

popped up their heads at the sound. How sorry they felt for Thumbelina! They decided they would try to help her, and so they all gathered around the water lily stem and nibbled away at it. Soon, it was gnawed in two. Away went the leaf, swept off down the stream.

Thumbelina drifted along in the sunshine, happy to be far from the toads. A lovely butterfly fluttered around her and came to rest on the leaf. Thumbelina undid the sash from around her waist and fastened one end of it to the butterfly, tying the other end to the leaf. That way, she could travel along even faster.

Just then, a big beetle swooped down and

grabbed Thumbelina, and flew off with her into a tree. She was very frightened, but the beetle was kind to her. He set her down on a large green leaf and told her how pretty she was – until all the other beetles arrived.

"What do you mean, she's pretty? She's only got two legs!" scoffed one.

"She hasn't got any feelers!" said another.

"She looks like a human being – really ugly," sneered a third.

Then the beetle changed his mind about Thumbelina. He picked her up again and flew down out of the tree. He left her sitting on a daisy, crying.

All summer long, poor Thumbelina lived alone in the woods. She wove herself a

hammock of grass beneath a big burdock leaf for shelter. She ate honey from the flowers and drank the morning dew.

But then the winter came. Snow began to fall and Thumbelina shivered with cold. The big burdock leaf withered with all the other plants and flowers, and Thumbelina had to search for new shelter.

In a nearby grain field she came across a little field mouse, who was very kind and took pity on Thumbelina. "You can live with me in my house," the tiny creature said. "All I ask is that you keep my house clean and tidy and tell me stories, for I love stories."

So Thumbelina did as the field mouse asked and she was comfortable and content.

A few days passed and the field mouse's friend, Mr Mole, came to visit. The mole was totally charmed by Thumbelina. He didn't really know how pretty she was, because he couldn't see very well, but he was bewitched by her sweet voice. He invited Thumbelina and the field mouse to come and visit him whenever they wanted.

Thumbelina didn't want to go underground, but the field mouse insisted. So a few days later they set off through the

tunnel to Mr Mole's house. They had got halfway when they came across a dead swallow on the ground. Thumbelina was sad and wondered how he had come to be there.

All the time Thumbelina was at Mr Mole's, she couldn't stop thinking about the poor swallow who should have been out in the open air, in the winter sunshine. That night she crept back down the tunnel with a little coverlet to spread over him. She bent and kissed him… and heard a soft *thump, thump,* as if something were beating inside his chest. It was the bird's heart! He was not dead, only numb with cold. Thumbelina hurried to fetch him some water and soon the little bird was revived.

"Thank you, thank you," he gasped.

Thumbelina looked after the swallow in secret all through the winter. Then, when spring arrived, Mr Mole announced that he was going to marry her. "You are lucky," the field mouse told her, "for he is very rich."

But Thumbelina wept as though her heart would break. She could not bear the thought of living underground, never to be out in the warm sunshine again.

"I am strong enough to leave now," the swallow told her. "Climb on my back and I will take you away with me."

"Oh yes, please!" said Thumbelina.

So up they soared, over forests and lakes and mountains, far away from Mr Mole and

the darkness of his underground home.

At length they came to a warm country, and a blue lake in a magnificent garden, where there was a palace of dazzling white marble. "Choose one of the flowers in the garden," said the swallow, "and I will put you down in it to rest."

Thumbelina chose one of the loveliest large white flowers. To her surprise, in the centre of it there was a little man with bright shining wings, wearing a golden crown. He was the spirit of the flower. There was a spirit living in every flower, but he was king of them all.

Thumbelina and the flower king fell in love with each other at once. They were soon

married, and the best wedding gift was a pair of wings for Thumbelina, so she could flutter from flower to flower just like her husband. Everyone rejoiced – especially the swallow.

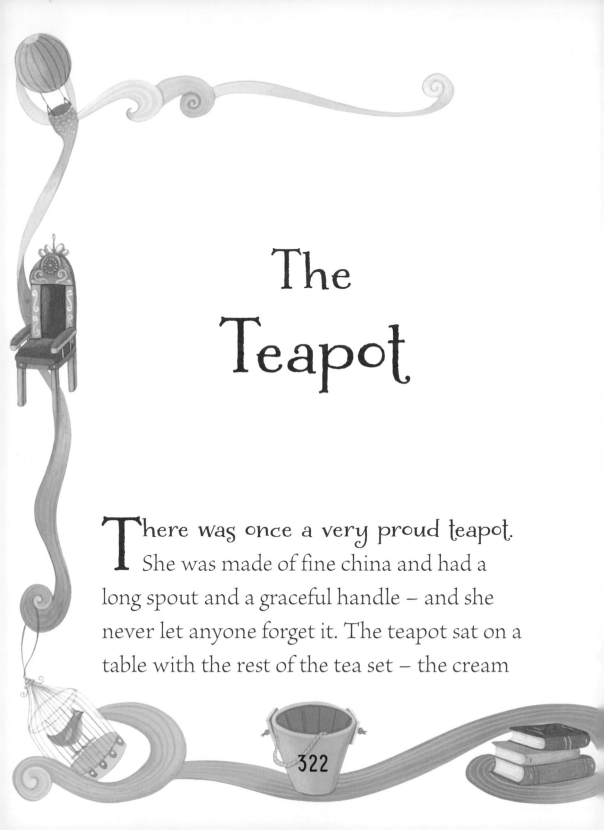

The Teapot

There was once a very proud teapot. She was made of fine china and had a long spout and a graceful handle – and she never let anyone forget it. The teapot sat on a table with the rest of the tea set – the cream

jug, the sugar bowl and the teacups and saucers – and she talked about her delicate, beautiful design all the time. However, the teapot never spoke about her lid, for that had a crack and a couple of chips in it. The teapot didn't want to point out her faults to others, so she kept quiet about those. But she went on and on and on about how beautiful the rest of her was.

"The cups have handles, like me," she would say to herself, "and the sugar bowl has a lovely round tummy, just like me. But even though the cream jug has a little lip, nobody has an actual spout – especially not a beautiful long one like mine – and so that makes me the queen of the tea table. The sugar bowl and the cream jug are like my maids, helping to serve the tea, but I am the most important one. Without me, everyone would go thirsty! Inside my tummy, I turn tasteless boiling water into a refreshing drink. The people could drink their tea out of glasses or bowls, so the teacups aren't of that much value. But without me – why, no one could drink tea at all!"

Now the cream jug, the sugar bowl and the teacups and saucers were very tired of hearing the teapot talk in this way –

especially when they knew full well that her lid was cracked and chipped!

"Who does she think she is?" the cream jug protested.

"Yes, how can she talk about being the most important of us when her lid is all damaged like that," scoffed the sugar bowl. "I've got a lid too – and mine isn't cracked or chipped!"

"And our handles are just as good as hers," piped up a teacup.

As the teapot boasted on and on, they sighed to each other, for they knew that everyone in the tea set was special in their own way. They all had an equally important role to play. At teatime, each one of them

was part of a team that worked together.

Then one teatime, the person pouring out the tea dropped the teapot! She fell to the floor, her spout broke in half and her handle snapped off. She lay in a faint on the carpet, while tea ran out of her. Once the other members of the tea set had got over the shock, they couldn't help but burst out laughing!

That was the last they saw of that teapot, for people hurried to clean up the broken mess and took her away. "Good riddance," the cream jug whispered with relief, as the teapot was carried out into the kitchen.

There, the broken teapot was examined. "Glue won't fix this," somebody said.

The Teapot

"We could use it as a plant pot instead," suggested somebody else.

So that's what they did. They filled the teapot with earth and then planted a flower bulb in it. The teapot was pleased, for now she had a heart. "I have never had a living heart until now," she said to herself. "I must be even more important than ever." The bulb pulsed with energy and power. It sprouted and grew, and thoughts and feelings swelled inside the teapot like she had never known before. Then a flower appeared, and everybody admired it and said how beautiful it was.

So the teapot was very happy sitting on the kitchen windowsill, with thoughts and

feelings and a pretty red flower to love.

And the cream jug, sugar bowl and cups and saucers welcomed a brand new teapot on to the tea table, who was modest and polite and fitted into the tea set very well.

The Daisy

Once upon a time, there stood a house in the countryside with a lovely garden. Lots of beautiful flowers grew within the garden, but there were pretty wildflowers outside the fence, too. One of them was a little white daisy, which stood in a patch of lush green grass by the roadside. The sun shone just as warmly on the daisy near the ditch as it did on the tulips and roses and wallflowers inside the garden, so the daisy was just as happy as they were.

One day the daisy was contentedly looking up into the bright sky, admiring a lark who was soaring and singing above her.

"I am sure that pretty lark must fly across and visit the bright garden flowers," she said to herself. "How lucky they are!" But just then, the lark turned and sailed down towards her. The little bird danced around the daisy and sang, "How soft the grass is here! And what a lovely little flower, with

gold in her heart and silver on her dress!"

The bird kissed the daisy with his beak, sang to her, and then flew up again into the bright blue sky. The daisy was so overjoyed, she didn't know what to think for the rest of the day.

That night, the daisy dreamt of the lark, dancing around her and singing. Next morning, as she woke up and stretched out her petals towards the sun, she wondered whether the little bird would come and see her again.

Then she heard his voice – but this time his song was sad and hopeless.

The Daisy

The poor lark had been caught! He was trapped in a cage inside the house, hanging by an open window.

How the little daisy wished she could help him! But what could she do? She quite forgot how beautiful the world was and how warmly the sun shone. All she could think of was the poor, unhappy bird…

Suddenly two little boys came out of the garden, one with a penknife in his hand. They went straight to the little daisy, and said: "Here we can cut a fine piece of turf for the lark." Then one of them began to cut out a square patch of grass right around her.

"Pull that daisy out," said the other boy. The daisy began to tremble with fear.

"No, leave it there," the first boy said. "It looks pretty." He picked up the square of earth, with the daisy still rooted in the middle, and he carried it inside the house and put it in the lark's cage.

The little bird was beating his wings against the bars of his prison. "Water!" he gasped. "You have forgotten to give me any water!" But the boys didn't understand what he was saying and just went away.

The desperate lark thrust his beak into the cool turf to refresh himself a little – and he

The Daisy

noticed the daisy. He kissed her with his beak and said, "My lovely little friend. We both need the sunshine and open air to live. I am afraid we will both just wither away in here!"

'If I could only help him and comfort him!' thought the daisy. She couldn't even move a leaf with no breeze or sunlight, but her beautiful scent seemed to cheer the lark a little.

By evening, the little bird no longer had the energy to beat his wings against the cage. He sat on the square of grass and his head drooped. The daisy couldn't fold her leaves and go to sleep, as she had done the night before. So she too bowed down, sorrowful and sick.

Next morning, when the boys came back to the cage, they found both the lark and the daisy dead. The poor lark's head rested on the daisy's petals and one of her leaves rested

on his breast. The boys were terribly upset when they realized that they were the cause. They took the bird and the flower outside and laid them under a tree together, out in the open air where they belonged. But the bird and the flower no longer cared nor minded – for they were happy in heaven.

The Wild Swans

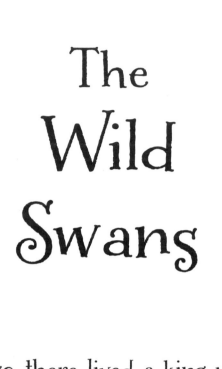

Long ago, there lived a king who had eleven sons and a little daughter, Eliza. Sadly, their mother died and after a while, the king married again.

His new bride was evil and hated the

children. She bewitched the king so he no longer noticed them. Then she sent Eliza away to live with a woodcutter in a shack in the forest. Finally, she pointed her bony finger at the princes and cried: "Fly out into the world and be gone!" The princes became magnificent wild swans. They flew out of the palace windows and off over the forest, away to the sea.

Years passed and poor Eliza longed for her family every day. The woodcutter told her what had happened to her brothers and, when she was fifteen, she made up her mind to search for them.

Eliza wandered through the forest for many days, until she came to the wide sea.

She felt as though she had reached the world's end.

When the sun was setting, Eliza suddenly saw eleven wild swans with crowns on their heads come flying across the water. She hid behind some rocks. The swans landed as the sun disappeared below the horizon. Then they vanished and in their places stood eleven handsome princes – Eliza's brothers! She raced to them and they all wept with joy.

"The queen enchanted us," the princes explained to Eliza. "While it is daylight, we must fly about as wild swans. But as soon as the sun sets, we become human once more. The queen has banished us to live in a country which lies across this ocean – we can

only come back here to our homeland once every year, to glimpse our father in the castle. Tomorrow, we must journey back across the sea. Will you come with us?"

"Oh yes, please," sighed Eliza.

The princes spent the night weaving a net of willow bark and reeds. Then at sunrise, Eliza lay in it and the princes, transformed back into swans, lifted it in their beaks and flew with her across the sea.

On they soared, until they reached a beautiful land. After sunset, the princes showed Eliza their home – a cave filled with thick moss, like a soft green carpet.

That night, Eliza had the strangest dream. A fairy came to her and told her how to free

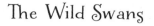

her brothers. "You must weave stinging nettles into eleven shirts, to cover your brothers," the fairy explained. "But you must use your bare hands, even though the nettles will sting them. And you must not speak a word until you are finished..."

The moment Eliza woke, she rushed out of the cave to begin her work. Her brothers were very shocked, especially because she could not talk, but they knew she must be up to something. After two weeks, one shirt was finished. Then Eliza began the second...

That day, while the swans were off flying, a pack of hunting dogs burst through the trees, closely followed by nobles on galloping horses. Eliza fled in terror back into the cave, but the most handsome man came and found her. He was a prince – and he had never seen a more beautiful girl. "Who are you?" he asked Eliza gently. But of course, she could not say a word.

The prince took Eliza and lifted her onto his horse, then galloped her back to the castle to look after her.

When the ladies-in-waiting had bathed Eliza and dressed her in royal robes, she looked dazzlingly beautiful. But her face was sadder than ever. Then the prince led her to her bedroom. It was decorated green, just like the cave, and in it were her nettles and the shirt she had already woven. Eliza kissed the prince joyfully.

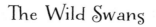

Days went by and Eliza fell as deeply in love with the kind prince as he was with her. He soon announced to everyone that they were getting married.

The people rejoiced – except for the prince's chief priest, the archbishop. "This wild girl from the forest who cannot speak must be a witch," he whispered into the prince's ear. "She has put you under her spell." Yet the prince refused to listen.

How Eliza longed to tell her beloved prince what she was doing. But of course, she could not. She got on with her work in silence. Eventually, ten shirts were finished – but she did not have enough nettles for the eleventh. She knew that more grew out in the

churchyard – but how would she ask for them? It was no good, she would have to go and fetch them herself.

That night, Eliza slipped away to the churchyard. There, a terrifying sight met her eyes – a coven of witches sat hunched over the tombstones, stirring up evil spells. Eliza hurried past them, then gathered some nettles and dashed back to the castle.

Little did she know, the archbishop had followed her and seen everything. "I knew it!" he murmured. "She's a witch!" He went straight to the prince and told him what he had seen. "See for yourself," he said. "Wait till this evening – maybe she will go to meet her witch friends again."

The Wild Swans

Eliza did indeed need more nettles and
that night slipped out again to the graveyard.
The archbishop and the prince followed her
at a distance – and unfortunately it did look
as though she was meeting the witches.

The prince felt heartbroken. The
punishment for being a witch was to be

burned at the stake! But there was nothing he could do. He had to follow his own laws, even though he loved Eliza deeply.

The next morning, soldiers came to arrest Eliza. They allowed her to bring the eleven nettle shirts as they led her to a big bonfire. All the people stood sadly around, for they could not believe that the lovely Eliza was a witch. But the archbishop seemed pleased as he strode over to light the flames.

All at once, there was a rush of air. Eleven mighty wild swans came flying around Eliza, beating the archbishop back with their wings. Eliza threw a nettle shirt over each one.

To everyone's amazement, the swans immediately disappeared and eleven

handsome princes stood there instead. However, the youngest had a swan's wing instead of one arm, for Eliza had not quite managed to finish one sleeve.

"Now I may speak!" Eliza cried. "I am innocent!" And she and her brothers quickly explained everything.

The prince ordered that the wicked archbishop should be hauled away to his deepest, darkest dungeon. He and Eliza were married in a magnificent wedding, and they brought her brothers to live with them in the castle, happily ever after.

Who was the Luckiest?

Once upon a time, a rose bush
stood in a garden.

"What beautiful roses!" said the sunshine.
"They are my children, I kissed them to life."

"No," said the dew. "They are my children,

because I gave them my tears to drink."

"I am their mother," said the rose bush firmly. "But you two are very special aunties."

"Our lovely rose children!" the rose bush, the dew and the sunshine all sighed. They wished the roses all the luck in the world. But who would turn out to be the luckiest in their life?

At that moment, a very sad lady came through the garden. She was a mother whose daughter had recently died. She picked the youngest rosebud, which was

351

just opening, for she thought it was the most beautiful of all. Then she kissed it and took it to lie on her little daughter's grave.

The rosebud trembled with joy. "I have been chosen as this special gift," she whispered. "Surely I am far luckier than my sisters."

But it wasn't long before another woman came walking into the garden. She caught sight of the largest, full-blown rose. She knew that with one more warm day, or one more dewy morning, its petals would fall to the ground. So the woman picked it and took it home to dry it out. Then she put it in a bowl with other dried flowers to make sweet-smelling potpourri.

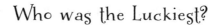

"What a wonderful honour," sighed the rose happily. "It must be me who is the luckiest, surely."

Then two young men came strolling through the garden. One was a painter and the other was a poet. Each of them picked a lovely rose. The painter created a picture of his rose. It was so lifelike that it could have been mistaken for the rose's reflection in a mirror. "In this way the rose will live on for a long time, while all the others fade and die," said the painter.

"Ah, now I have had the best luck of all," whispered the rose.

The poet looked at the rose that he had chosen and wrote a poem about it.

"No, I am definitely the luckiest," this rose decided. "A painting on canvas will fade one day, but the words of a poem can live on in people's minds forever."

Then into the garden came the gardener, who chose a young rose to go at the centre of a lovely bouquet of other flowers. The gardener gave it to a young man, who took it to a ballet at the theatre that night.

At the end of the performance, the ballerina came back on to the stage and curtseyed gracefully, to thunderous applause. A shower of flowers and bouquets came raining down around her, thrown by the audience. The young man threw his bouquet too. As it flew through the air, the rose

danced for joy. It sprang so high that when it landed on the stage, it snapped right off its stem!

The rose rolled into the wings, where a stagehand picked it up. He took it home and set it in a glass of water. Then he took it to his sick grandmother's bedside.

"I know you have no stem," the feeble old

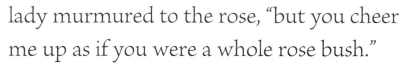

lady murmured to the rose, "but you cheer me up as if you were a whole rose bush."

The rose swelled with joy and pride. "I am the luckiest, without a doubt," she decided.

So every rose had its own story. And every rose was sure that it was the luckiest one.

"I am very lucky too," said the wind, "for I can travel far and wide, to many different places. I know the story of all the roses and I can spread it throughout the world. Perhaps it is I who am the luckiest of all…"

So tell me, what do you think? You must say, for I have said enough.

Little Tuck

There was once a young boy whose name was Charlie – but everyone called him Tuck. One day, his mother was so busy that she asked him to look after his little sister, Grace, who was much younger than he was. Tuck loved his sister and didn't mind this at all. But there was one problem: he had homework to do at the same time. He had to learn the capital cities of all the countries of the world, for a geography test the next day. So Tuck ended up sitting with his little sister on his lap, singing her all the songs he knew, while glancing into his geography book at the same time.

As you can imagine, Tuck did not get on very well with his learning. As soon as his mother had finished her work and could keep an eye on Grace once more, he ran up to his bedroom and settled down to study his geography book.

But then there came a call from Tuck's

mother downstairs. "Through the window I can see the old washerwoman from down the lane," she shouted up. "She's struggling to carry a bucket of water from the well. Be a good boy, Tuck, and go and help her."

So Tuck jumped up and ran to help the old woman.

By the time he got home again, dusk was falling and it was too dim inside the cottage to read any longer. Tuck's family were too poor to afford candles, so all he could do was go to bed. He lay there, thinking about the countries of the world and their capital cities. He certainly hadn't done enough studying, but of course, he couldn't carry on now.

Instead, Tuck put his geography book

under his pillow, because he had heard one of his friends say that if you did that, the information sank into your brain while you slept. Tuck wasn't really sure that that was true, but he thought it was worth a try...

Tuck lay there, thinking and thinking... then all of a sudden he felt a kiss on his forehead. He wasn't sure if he was awake or just dreaming, but he felt as if

the old washerwoman was there, looking at him kindly. "You helped me and now I'll help you," she said. Then all at once the book under his pillow began to wriggle around.

It was a koala that came crawling out. "I'm from Canberra, Australia," she said. And then she told him all about her city and how many people there were in it.

"Cockadoodledo!" cried out something from under the bed. It was a Belgian rooster. "I'm from Brussels," he said, and he told the little boy very proudly that the Belgian coast tram was the longest tramway line in the world.

Tuck realized he was no longer lying in bed. All of a sudden, he was on horseback,

galloping along a riverbank by a forest. "I am a Canadian horse from Ottawa," his steed snorted, and went on to tell him all about the Native American tribes who first lived in that land.

And so animals from all the countries in the world kept coming to Tuck and teaching him all about their lands – although he was actually lying in his bed the whole time.

Then all at once the animals vanished.
Tuck began to dream that he was with his
sister, flying through the air – but Grace had
grown up and become a beautiful lady.
Together they flew over snowy mountains

and hot deserts and wide seas. "Look at the world, little Tuck," Grace said as they soared. "One day you will explore it all and you will become rich and famous."

And then Tuck woke up. It was broad daylight and he couldn't remember anything – although he felt as though he had had a very strange dream indeed.

With a start, he remembered his geography test, and so he sprang out of bed and pulled his book out from under his pillow. He hurried downstairs, and sat at the breakfast table and pored over it. To his astonishment, he knew every capital city and facts about them without hesitation!

Just then, the old washerwoman passed by

the window. She turned and smiled at Tuck and said good morning to him. "May all your dreams come true, my dear," she said.

Little Tuck still couldn't remember what he had dreamed – but to his surprise, he came top in his geography test!

The
Days
of the
Week

The days of the week once wanted to stop working for a while and get together to have a party. However, each of the seven days had so much going on, all year round, that they had no time to spare. They

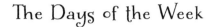

had to wait until an extra day came around –
the twenty-ninth of February, which only
happens once every four years, in a leap year.

On that day they planned to have a huge
celebration. They would have lots of nice
things to eat and drink, and make speeches
and tell jokes, and dance and sing, and
generally have a good time enjoying
themselves.

Each day of the week was to come in fancy
dress – whatever they chose. They each spent
ages deciding who to come as and what to
wear. They could hardly wait.

Finally, the twenty-ninth of February
arrived. It was at last time for the party!

Sunday, the leader of the days, came

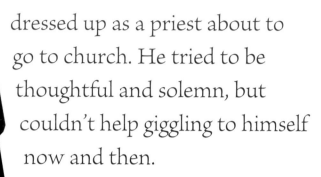

dressed up as a priest about to go to church. He tried to be thoughtful and solemn, but couldn't help giggling to himself now and then.

Monday – who was Sunday's younger brother – turned up next. He had decided to come dressed as a schoolboy, for he was the start of the working week. He looked very smart in his blazer and tie, and swung his schoolbag merrily.

Tuesday came dressed as a warrior, wearing a helmet and holding a

sword in his left hand. "Tuesday comes from the name of the Viking god of combat, Tyr," he explained. He brandished his weapon and roared, and he looked most fearsome indeed!

Wednesday turned up as a prince, with a golden crown perched on his head. "Surely I am the most important day," he joked. "The week is like a royal procession. Three days come before me, to announce that I am coming. And three days come after me, following behind like

369

my servants. You fellows are like my guards of honour!" And everyone laughed.

Thursday came dressed as a warrior, like Tuesday. He wore a sturdy metal belt, big gloves and a red beard. In his hand he carried a huge, heavy hammer. "I am named after the Viking god of thunder, Thor," he announced. "My magic belt doubles my mighty strength and I use my iron gloves to grip my magic hammer – a weapon so deadly that I can crush mountains with it!"

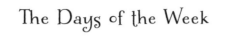

Friday was one of the two female days of the week. She was a beautiful young girl and she came dressed in a long robe, wearing a stunning necklace, with a soft feather cloak draped around her shoulders. "My name comes from the Viking goddess of love, Freya," she smiled. "My necklace, Brisingamen, was made by dwarfs and my cloak has magic powers so I can fly between worlds."

Saturday was the other female day – and the last to arrive. She was an older woman dressed as a housewife, carrying a broom and a bag of knitting. She brought a big plate of sandwiches with her. "Well, someone has to look after everybody," she laughed.

Then the party got underway – and a very good time was had by all. It was certainly a celebration worth waiting for!

The Travelling Companion

Once there was a young man
called John, whose family sadly all died.
He did not want to stay at home alone, so he
set off into the world to see where the road
would take him.

As evening fell on the first day of his travels, the weather turned dreadfully stormy. John slipped inside a little church to take shelter. There before the altar was an open coffin and in it lay a dead man, waiting to be buried the next day. John wasn't at all frightened. He was sure that dead people can't do any harm. It was living people that he was more worried about.

John gave a coin to light a candle, then knelt and prayed for the stranger – that God would forgive his sins and welcome him into heaven. Then John settled down in a corner and spent the night there, keeping the dead man company.

Early next morning, John set off once

more. He had just strode through a forest
when he heard a man call from behind.
"Hey there, friend, do you mind
if I travel along with you?"
"Not at all," said John.
The two men
talked as they
walked, and soon
came to like each
other very much.
They journeyed
on for many miles,
until at last they
caught sight of a
town, with a great
palace in the middle.

John and his companion did not enter the town straight away. First they stopped at an inn, to wash and change into clean clothes.

The innkeeper told them that the king was a good man, but his daughter, the princess, was an evil witch. She had declared that any man might try to win her hand in marriage. All he had to do was guess what she was thinking about. If he knew the answer, he would be her husband. But if he didn't know the answer, she muttered a wicked spell and he vanished, never to be seen again!

The innkeeper explained that sadly, hundreds of young men had disappeared in this way. The king was deeply upset about it, but his daughter's powers were so strong that

he could do nothing to stop her.

Just then, John and his companion heard people shouting "Hooray! Hooray!" outside the inn. They hurried to see what was happening. The princess was passing by – and she was so beautiful that everyone forgot how wicked she was and cheered her!

John could scarcely catch his breath, he was so stunned by her. "I must go to the palace and see if I can win her hand in marriage," he decided. "Surely it can't be true that she is a wicked witch!"

The innkeeper and John's travelling companion both tried to persuade him not to go, but John would not listen. So the next day, the travellers walked to the palace.

The king was very sorry to see them, for he did not want John to vanish, like all the other young men. But John would not be put off. It was arranged that he would visit the palace again the following morning to guess what the princess was thinking of. And John fairly skipped for joy back to the inn, thinking only of how lovely the princess was.

As night began to draw in, the travelling companion brought John a glass of beer. "Now we must drink the health of the princess!" he said. But once John had had only a few sips, he felt so sleepy that he sank down over the table, snoring. Then John's friend opened the window. Wings suddenly sprouted from his shoulders and he flew off

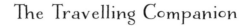

over the rooftops to the palace, where he perched on a ledge outside the princess's bedroom window.

At a quarter to twelve the window opened and the princess flew out. She had grown wings too! John's travelling companion made himself invisible, so he could follow her.

The princess soared away to a high mountain. She knocked on the mountainside and, with a rumble like thunder, it opened up. In went the princess and in went the invisible travelling companion after her.

They entered a long corridor built of silver and gold. The walls were lined with flowers which had snakes for stems and flames for petals. Eventually, it opened up into a vast

hall. In the middle was a throne made out of bones, and on the throne sat an old, evil-eyed sorcerer. The princess sank low in a curtsey to him and he kissed her forehead. "Think of my golden crown," he instructed her, "the young man will never guess that.

And when he fails, don't forget to send him straight to me, so I may eat him…"

The princess curtseyed again and set off home, flying through the night air.

But the travelling companion did not follow her straight away. Instead, he crept close to the sorcerer and yanked the golden crown from his head. Then away he flew, leaving the sorcerer howling in a fit of rage behind him.

Next morning, John presented himself before the princess, with his travelling companion at his side. As he stood, puzzling hard over what she could be thinking of, John felt his friend push something into his hand. John held out his hand and opened it – and there was the sorcerer's crown!

The princess turned chalk-white and trembled from head to foot, but there was nothing she could do. His guess was right. Finally she sighed and said: "You are my master now. Our wedding will be held this evening."

Then the king jumped for joy, and everyone joined in the rejoicing.

That night, there was the most splendid wedding ever seen. Yet the princess scowled and was steely-eyed, for she was still an evil witch and had no love for John at all. When the festivities were coming to an end, and John and the princess were about to go to bed, John's travelling companion gave him a little bottle of liquid. "Put three drops in the princess's drink and then hold on to her tight," he said.

So that's what John did. To his astonishment, the princess turned into a black swan, struggling to get free. But John held tight and the black swan turned into a white swan, struggling even harder. John held tighter still – and then the white swan changed back into the beautiful princess. She was even more lovely than before!

With tears in her eyes, the princess thanked John, for at last she had been freed from the sorcerer's spell which had made her so wicked.

The next morning, John's travelling

companion wished him goodbye. "Your place is here now but I must move on," he said. "For I am the dead man you prayed for in church and now I have repayed your kindness." And with one last smile, he disappeared.

Alas, John never saw his faithful friend again, but he and the princess lived happily ever after.